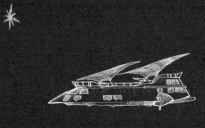

TOM ANGLEBERGER

AMULET BOOKS
NEW YORK

THE SURPRISE ATTACK OF JABBA THE PUPPETT

AN ORIGAMI YODA BOOK

Cataloging-in-Publication Data has been applied for and may be obtained from the Library of Congress.

ISBN: 978-1-4197-0858-9

Text copyright © 2013 Tom Angleberger
Book design by Melissa J. Arnst

Printed and bound in U.S.A.
10 9 8 7 6 5 4 3 2 1

Amulet Books are available at special discounts when purchased in quantity for premiums and promotions as well as fundraising or educational use. Special editions can also be created to specification. For details, contact specialsales@abramsbooks.com or the address below.

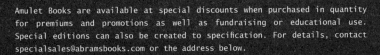

ABRAMS
THE ART OF BOOKS SINCE 1949

115 West 18th Street
New York, NY 10011
www.abramsbooks.com

THIS BOOK IS DEDICATED TO THE PEOPLE OF
LUCASFILM, PAST AND PRESENT . . . WITH SPECIAL
THANKS TO THE ALWAYS AWESOME PUBLISHING
DEPARTMENT, THE SENSATIONAL CLONE WARS
TEAM, EVERYONE WORKING TO MAKE THE NEW
MOVIES, AND, OF COURSE, GEORGE LUCAS! STAR
WARS IS AN AMAZING STORY, AND I AM HONORED
TO GET TO DOODLE IN THE MARGINS.

WE'RE REALLY READY

BY TOMMY

Me and Kellen knew we would be starting a new case file when Dwight got back.

We just didn't know what it would be about.

I mean, you never, never know what to expect from Dwight.

He and his Origami Yoda used the Force to help out a bunch of us at school. OR DID HE REALLY?

But then he and Origami Yoda were beaten by Darth Paper and Harvey. OR WERE THEY REALLY?

Then he went away to this weird brainwashy

school and left an Origami Chewbacca to help us. OR DID HE REALLY?

Then he turned normal and gave up Origami Yoda. OR DID HE REALLY? Well, actually, yes, he really did, but we were able to save him and convince him to come back to our school after his suspension was over.

It's all those "REALLY?"s that make me write these case files. Because, like I said, you never know what Dwight is going to do, and lots of times even when he's doing it you still don't know what he's really doing.

So that's why I was ready to start this case file the minute Dwight walked back through the doors of McQuarrie Middle School. I couldn't wait to find out what he was REALLY going to do this time . . .

THE RETURN OF THE DWIGHT

BY TOMMY

Today was January 6, the first day of the spring semester.

We found out that there are going to be a lot of weird changes at school.

Judging by how excited Principal Rabbski was about them, they could not possibly be good. And judging by the posters that were going up around school—"Get Ready for a Fun Time with FunTime!!!!"—they're probably really, really bad.

RABBSKI

So everybody was waiting for a special assembly that was going to happen right after homeroom, when Rabbski was finally going to tell us what FunTime was all about.

But first, we figured, there would be The Return of the Dwight. He was kicked out for the fall semester. This was the start of the spring semester. And he HAD said he was coming back.

So . . . would he have Origami Yoda with him? Or was he going to wait a few days for that? Would he be happy to see us? Would he say, "Hey, everybody, thanks for saving me from the brainwashing?" Or would he just say, "Purple," and not look at anybody, like he does sometimes?

Whatever he did, I was ready to write about it in this case file. And Kellen was ready to doodle about it. (And of course Harvey was ready to complain about it.)

When I got to school and Sara told me that Dwight wasn't on the bus with her this

READY

READY

READY!

morning, I was a little worried that he had changed his mind about coming back. Or that his mother had changed it for him.

But then Mike came running into the library to say that he saw Dwight and his mom going into the office. That made sense; there's probably some kind of paperwork she has to fill out. Maybe he needed to be re-enrolled for the spring semester or something.

And I'm sure Principal Rabbski wanted a chance to warn him about "not disrupting the learning environment."

"Well?" I asked Mike. "Did you talk to him? Did he talk to you?"

"No, I didn't have a chance. They were right outside the office. His mom was down on her knees, looking right in his face. She said, 'Are you SURE you want to do this, honey?' and he nodded his head and she was hugging him and stuff, so I just kept walking. But guess what he was wearing?"

"What?"

DWIGHT'S MOM
→

"His old 'Biggie Size Your Combo for Just 39 Cents' shirt!"

That was a good sign. (I think.)

"And his cape."

That didn't seem like such a good sign.

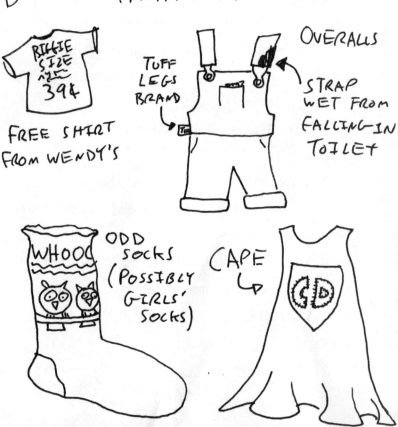

DWIGHT'S FASHION ACCESSORIES:

BIGGIE SIZE ~1~ 39¢

FREE SHIRT FROM WENDY'S

TUFF LEGS BRAND

OVERALLS

STRAP WET FROM FALLING IN TOILET

WHOOO

ODD SOCKS (POSSIBLY GIRLS' SOCKS)

CAPE

CD

THE FIRST PERSON TO TALK TO DWIGHT

BY JEN

Tommy, I'm actually sitting down to write you an e-mail instead of just a text this time. Because of course I feel terrible about Dwight getting kicked out of school, because a lot of it was my fault for letting Harvey talk me into telling on Dwight . . . but you know all about that.

Anyway, I had been practicing an apology and was waiting for a good chance to talk to him. Then all of a sudden, there he was!

I'm in Miss Bauer's homeroom, you know, and we were on our way to the cafeteria for the assembly about all the new FunTime classes. (Which, by the way, are going to

MISS BAUER

suck.) We passed the office and Dwight just popped out and started walking along with us . . . right next to me!

First thing I noticed, of course, was that he was wearing his cape again. But I wasn't about to mention it!

"Oh, Dwight, I am so glad you're back!" I told him. "I am so, so, so sorry for what happened. I—"

But he cut me off!

You know how Dwight is usually all "whlluuu, whlluuu, whlluuuu"? You know, spacy and mumbly and stuff? Well, he was totally the opposite of that!

"Thanks, Jen. It wasn't your fault anyway," he said. "But we've got no time for all that now. We must use the information in this assembly to plan our attack!"

I kind of panicked when he said "attack." Was he starting to say scary stuff again? I had forgotten that I was sometimes a little afraid of him. Was I going to have to tell on him again? On his first day?

"Uh, Dwight, did you really mean to say 'attack'? Attack what? You're not going to attack Harvey or something, are you?"

"No, we'll need Harvey on our side. You, too, Jen. We'll need everybody."

"Everybody? But what are you going to . . . uh . . . attack?"

"FunTime! It must be destroyed!" he said, staring straight ahead. "I only hope that when Rabbski's speech is analyzed, a weakness can be found. It's not over yet."

"SHHHH!" shushed Miss Bauer. "You should be walking, not talking."

And then we were at the assembly and that was it. I will just point out that Dwight listened to absolutely every word Rabbski said and didn't even fidget much while she was talking!

Harvey's Comment

Well, even I have to admit that I'm glad he's back. The rest of you guys are so boring. So, welcome back, Dwight!

But the cape? Not so much.

He wore that for most of fifth grade. I hope he's not going to tell us to call him Captain Dwight again!

My Comment: If the cape is helping him stay focused on destroying FunTime, then I'm all for it, because FunTime is . . . is . . . well, I'll just let Rabbski explain it in her own words .

RABBSKI'S SPEECH AT THE ASSEMBLY

BY MS. LOUGENE RABBSKI

(AS RECORDED BY KELLEN'S RECORDER THINGY)

I am holding up my hand! When the hand goes up, your mouths go shut, your eyes are up front! You guys should know that by now . . . Harvey! Harvey! It is time to STOP talking. Thank you!

Okay . . .

Now . . . uh . . . okay, now where is it? Okay . . .

I recently had the toughest moment in my entire career as an educator. I had to take down the banner in our lobby that says

McQuarrie students have passed our state Standards tests.

For eight years in a row, McQuarrie Middle School students met the minimum standards on the state tests!

Last year we did not meet the minimum standards. Test scores at McQuarrie were the lowest in the county. And I had to take that banner down.

Now, I know that you kids are the BEST students in this county, right? Right?

So, we are going to prove it!

We're going to join together and get those scores up!

We are going to pass those minimum requirements this year! And put that banner back up where it belongs!

But it's going to take a lot of hard work— and, yes, some sacrifices.

As some of you may know, there will be no electives this semester. I was always proud of what you kids did in your elective classes—

HAPPY VIKING

SAD VIKING

PIZZA BAGEL PRIDE!

← GENUINE LEATHER

your artwork, your band and choral concerts, your model rockets, pizza bagels, and stamped leather key chains. And we hope that many of these activities can continue after school . . . on Wednesdays and alternate Thursdays.

And I know that you will all be as sorry as I am that we will not be able to take our spring field trip to Washington, D.C., this year. But—

I am holding up my hand! I am holding up my hand! You should not be talking. Thank you!

I know you are all disappointed. As I said, I am, too. BUT we are hoping—if progress is being made—to have a half-day mini-trip for each grade, possibly to Greenhill Plantation.

RABBSKI'S SILENT VIKING HAND SIGNAL

My hand is up! Your mouths should be shut! If your attitude about Greenhill Plantation is THAT bad, you can sit in ISS while the rest of your friends go!

Okay, uh . . . But, we can't allow all these things to take too much time away from our CORE curriculum: math, science, language

GREENHILL PLANTATION.

COW   POOP (everywhere)

GREEN HILL ↓

K-MART

arts, history. These are the subjects at the heart of our school . . . and on our state Standards tests. They are the fundamental building blocks of your education.

We need to FOCUS on these FUNDAMENTALS if we want to improve our scores and get that banner back up!

So . . . the Lucas County Board of Education has partnered with Edu-Fun Educational Products to do just that! We will begin using their new, highly effective educational system called "TIME to FOCUS on the FUNdamentals," or FunTime for short.

Instead of going to your elective classes each day, you'll be assigned to a new classroom, where you'll use the FunTime system to prepare for your upcoming state Standards of Learning tests.

BORED!

THE FUNTIME MENACE

BY TOMMY

None of that was a real surprise. Last semester, Cassie and Sara had figured out that the chorus teacher was leaving and there wouldn't be any more chorus classes. Then Kellen found out the same thing about art class. Then Rabbski sent a letter to all our parents, telling them that "elective" classes were out and test-prep classes were in. And there had been rumors that the field trip was getting canceled. (But the threat of making us go to Greenhill Plantation AGAIN was new . . .

ALL THE BEST CLASSES NOW CANCELED.

and particularly fiendish! We got dragged there so many times in elementary school. And once you've seen it, you've seen it. It's just an old house with ropes across the doors of all the rooms so you can only peek in, and when you peek in—whee!—old junk!)

We had all spent a lot of time complaining about not getting to take our electives. (I had signed up for LEGO robots with Mr. Randall! And Sara!) But none of us realized just how bad things were going to be. Well, I guess Dwight did. Dwight knew. Or maybe it was Origami Yoda who knew. Either way . . . it was bad.

When Rabbski was done, we were told to go to our second-period class, which normally would have been one of our electives, for "re-assignment" to a new classroom. I don't know about you, but the word "re-assignment" makes me think of something Empress Rabbski—oops, I mean Emperor Palpatine—would do to a prisoner.

ZAP!

So I went to Mr. Randall's room and Sara was there, and so were Lance and Quavondo. We would have had a great LEGO robot team!

But Mr. Randall told us not to sit down.

"I wish you guys could stay, but I have a whole room full of sixth-graders coming in here."

MR.
RANDALL

"Where are we supposed to go?" asked Sara.

"Well," said Mr. Randall, "let me just have a look at the world's worst-designed chart here . . ." He started flipping through a packet of papers.

"Sara, it looks like you'll be going to Mr. Stevens's room. Quavondo, you're also going to Stevens. Lance and Tommy, you'll be going to . . . Howell."

"Ha!" said Lance. "Go to Howell! That sounds about right."

It did sound right! In just one morning, I had gone from LEGOS with Sara to FunTime with Mr. Howell!

There was some good news, though. When I

got to Mr. Howell's room, Kellen was already there.

"Some lady I've never seen before was in the art room, and she told us to come here. Plus, a bunch of eighth-graders were going into the art room, which by the way doesn't have any art stuff in it at all! I want to know where my clay Jabba sculpture from last semester is!"

Then came Mike and Cassie.

We were all grumpy about various things, but I was trying to look on the bright side. Maybe it wasn't going to be TOO bad. A bunch of my best friends were here now. Maybe it would be a little bit of FUN™.

And then . . .

A shadow fell across the room . . .

A figure loomed in the doorway . . .

A being of infinite malice and darkness stood there . . .

A disturbance in the Force!

"Howell!" whispered Kellen.

It was Mr. Howell, our sixth-grade homeroom teacher, known for his evil deeds and hatred of all students, but especially me and Kellen.

"I don't like it any better than you do, Kellen," said Mr. Howell. "I had more than enough of your bad attitude last year. And I have a bad feeling your bad attitude is just going to be . . . badder . . . when you see this video."

Howell pointed a remote at a cart with a DVD player and a TV.

He pushed a button.

Laser beams shot out of the TV and blew up our brains.

No, not really. What really happened was worse! The TV came on and the DVD started . . .

And FunTime began!!!

Imagine, if you will, another world, another galaxy, where there is someone like Mr. Good Clean Fun, the guy with the monkey puppet who comes to our assembly and sings songs about how to blow your nose. But this other-galaxy

dude is actually worse—he lip-synchs all his songs and is named . . . Professor FunTime! And instead of a puppet, he has an animated, singing calculator.

And together they sang:

"FunTime! Every minute, every second will . . . help you FOCUS on the FUNdamentals!"

The weird dude said, "I'm Professor FunTime!"

And the calculator said, "And I'm Gizmo!"

"We're here to help you PREP for your big test!"

"What does 'PREP' stand for, Professor?"

"'Preparation and RE-view Period!'"

"Wouldn't that be 'PARP'?" asked Kellen.

"Please, Kellen, this is painful enough already," said Mr. Howell.

So then the Professor and Gizmo did a math problem. A real easy one like we learned three or four years ago in math class. Then they sang about it. Then they did it again. The exact same problem with the same numbers and everything. Then they sang AGAIN!

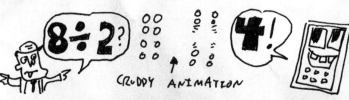

CRUDDY ANIMATION

"Okay, would the teacher now press pause and hand out the worksheets?" said the Professor, and he and Gizmo sat there blinking for a while until Mr. Howell woke up from a semi-stupor, found the remote, and paused them right in mid-blink.

Then Howell gave each of us a worksheet. At the top it said "FunTime™. Seventh-Grade Math Standards 0.1.1." At the bottom it said "Copyright Edu-Fun Educational Products."

The first thing on the worksheet was the exact same problem that the Professor had done on the video. Then there were nine more very similar problems. It took about twenty seconds to do the whole thing. Like I said, we all learned how to do these a long time ago.

When we were all done, Mr. Howell hit the play button and Gizmo went over the answers . . . very, very slowly . . . and showed us how to do each one . . . very, very slowly.

And then he sang!

Kellen whispered, "Thank Jar Jar, it's almost over!"

And then Professor FunTime said, "Great job, everybody! See . . . with a little PREP, you can go a long way! We'll see you tomorrow for more . . . FunTime!"

"Tomorrow?" I asked as I began to glimpse the DARK TRUTH!

"Oh, yes," said Mr. Howell. "And the next day and the next day and the next day. Every day until the test."

"When's that?"

"Sometime in May. So only about four and a half months . . ."

Kellen stood up and shouted, "NOOOOOOOOOOOO!"

SAVE US, YODA!

SAVE US, ORIGAMI YODA!

BY TOMMY

By the time we all met up in the cafeteria for lunch, we were all thinking the same thing: How is Origami Yoda going to get us out of this?

So far, Origami Yoda has gotten us out of all kinds of bad stuff and into all kinds of good stuff. So it was just natural to ask Dwight to ask Origami Yoda what to do.

Clearly, Dwight was ready for this. He hadn't even gotten lunch. I repeat, Dwight Tharp—who actually likes our school lunch, who actually

NO LUNCH!!!

ORIGAMI YODA!

CAPE!

LOVES our school lunch—was intentionally skipping it on his first day back.

He was just sitting there at the table with Origami Yoda. Waiting for us.

"Hey, Dwight, what are we gonna—"

"Patience . . . ," said Origami Yoda. "Wait for everyone we must."

"Okay, but you do know what to do, right?"

"Yes . . . ," said Origami Yoda. "Know I do . . . yes . . ."

Dwight has a bunch of different Yoda voices. None of them sound that much like Yoda, but you can often tell what sort of mood Origami Yoda is in. There's sort of the screechy normal voice, a dreamy future-telling voice, and then there's the scary, time-to-get-out-the-lightsaber voice. That's the one Origami Yoda was using now.

Sara, Rhondella, and Amy came and sat at their end of the table. Origami Yoda told them to wait, too. Then Mike, Lance, and Quavondo came. And finally, Harvey.

"We were waiting on Harvey?" complained Kellen. "Why?"

Origami Yoda cut him off.

"Now see you the perils of the FunTime Menace?"

"Yes," said Harvey. "It's like being in the Sarlacc pit and being slowly digested for a thousand years."

"Gross," said Rhondella.

"But accurate," said Sara.

"Well," said Lance. "Can you do something about it? Can you stop it?"

Origami Yoda shook his tiny paper head back and forth.

"Do that I cannot," he said.

"But you're Yoda! Yoda can do anything," said Mike.

"Hrmmm," said Origami Yoda. "No. Remember my failure in the Senate chamber. All-powerful I am not. Too strong this enemy is for one Jedi."

"So why are we sitting here listening to you, then?" asked Harvey.

"Because . . . the time has come to use what you have learned. Fold more origami you must. Join with Captain Dwight you must."

"Captain Dwight?" brayed Harvey.

"Yes! Join him you must. Only together can you withstand this enemy. An origami alliance you need."

"Geez . . . are you talking about an origami club or something?" said Rhondella. "I pass."

"No! More than a club you need. More is required of you than that. It is time for faithfulness . . . solidarity . . . courage . . . all the qualities of a Jedi."

"But for what?" Kellen and I asked at the same time.

Origami Yoda looked at each of us . . . even at Dwight. For a second I thought about how crazy it was, all of us sitting there staring at a finger puppet and then the finger puppet staring back and us watching while the finger puppet looked at the guy who owns the finger.

But something else told me it wasn't crazy. When Origami Yoda looked at me with his crinkly eyes, I knew what he was going to say. And I knew I was going to agree.

"Come the time has . . . ," Origami Yoda said slowly, "for rebellion."

"Snort," snorted Harvey.

Harvey's Comment

Captain Dwight? Captain? We just had to rescue the guy from a school because the kids were being too nice to him . . . and now all of a sudden he's Captain Dwight again?

My Comment: It is pretty weird. He's not acting like a superhero this time, more like Captain Rex. All business. Captain Dwight is almost the opposite of the Special Dwight we had to rescue. He's not in dreamland. He doesn't start babbling about the history of giant yo-yos or whatever. He's actually focused. Of course, he's still got a talking finger puppet, so no one is going to mistake him for normal.

CAPTAIN REX: ALL BUSINESS

ORDER 66 MORE FILE CABINETS.

HOLOCRON KEEPER.

THE PAPER REBELLION

BY MIKE, THE HOLOCRON KEEPER

Captain Dwight said, "Who wants to be the Holocron Keeper?" and I thought that would be awesome, because the real-life Holocron Keeper is this cool dude who works for Lucasfilm and who knows EVERYTHING about *Star Wars*.

But then Dwight handed me a spiral notebook. He had used an eraser to write/scratch HOLOCRON in white letters on the red cover.

"Uh, this is the Holocron?" I said.

"No, empty notebook it is," said Origami Yoda. "To record everything and MAKE IT a Holocron your mission is."

"Wait a minute!" said Tommy. "Isn't that what I do?"

"Do or do not, there is no try," said Origami Yoda.

"Uh, that doesn't answer my question!" said Tommy.

"AHEM . . . If you don't mind, we have a lot to get done," said Dwight. "Now, who is joining the rebellion? Raise your hands. Please write down the names of the members of the Rebel Alliance, Holocron Keeper."

So I did.

Dwight, Tommy, Kellen, Lance, Mike, Amy, Sara, Quavondo. Harvey and Rhondella did not raise their hands.

"I'm not raising my hand until I know what we're doing," said Harvey.

"We are forming an Origami Rebel Alliance," said Dwight. "We are breaking free from the Edu-Fun Empire. We will demand that we get our classes back, get to go on our field trip, and not have to fill out those worksheets or watch those dumb videos anymore."

I may be wrong, but this seemed like the first time I had ever heard Dwight make sense. I mean, it was a long sentence with verbs and nouns and not just "purple" and a bunch of weirdness.

HOWEVER, it didn't seem to make actual sense as far as being something we could actually do, though.

"How can we 'demand' anything?" said Harvey. "Remember, I went to a school board meeting last year and complained about the no-video-games-in-the-library rule and I couldn't even get them to listen to me, much less do what I asked."

"Yes, I remember that," said Dwight. "That was a bold action. But you stood alone. We will stand together."

"Stand together and do what?" asked Amy.

"Fail," croaked Origami Yoda.

"That's what I'm saying!" said Harvey.

"No . . . Failure a path to victory can be."

"Here we go with the jibber-jabber," said Harvey. "Next thing you know, Sara is going to get out her Fortune Cookie Wookiee!"

"WRRRRGGHHHH," said Sara, waving her taped-up Origami Chewbacca and Han Foldo.

"That means shut up, Harvey," said Han Foldo. "And it also means, Dwight, if you understand what Origami Yoda's saying, then let's hear it, kid."

"Okay, but remember: It's CAPTAIN Dwight," said Dwight. "The problem is that the average test scores for the whole school are too low, right? And Rabbski brought in FunTime to make the scores go up. Well, what if we make them go down?"

"How?"

"Fail the tests you must," said Origami Yoda.

"The Standards tests? You mean fail on purpose?"

"Purpose on," said Yoda.

"I see what he's saying," said Amy. "Let's say you would have gotten an 80 on the test. Instead you get a 0. That brings down the school average."

"How much?" asked Sara.

HUGE

bit

"Just a tiny bit," said Amy.

"Yes . . . a tiny bit by one student . . . a huge bit if by many!" said Origami Yoda.

"Huge bit?" said Harvey. "Isn't that an . . ."

"Shhhh!" hissed Kellen. "I totally see what he's saying! If we all agree to do this, then we can prevent FunTime from working!"

"Hmmm . . . How many of us will have to do it?" asked Sara.

"Not sure am I," said Origami Yoda. "Look to Amy for Jedi Math Skills we will."

"What? I'm not THAT good at math," said Amy.

"That good you are," said Origami Yoda. "Also, R2-D2 will help you."

Dwight pulled out this big brown envelope. He reached inside and got out a pack of fancy origami paper. He took out a sheet that had silver foil on one side and handed it to Amy. "You'll find the instructions in the case file Kellen and I made," said Dwight.

Then he pulled out a sheet with gold foil and gave it to Lance.

THESE ARENT THE FOILS YOU ARE LOOKING FOR...

FUTURE R2-D2

FUTURE C-3PO

"What's this for?"

"C-3PO."

"No way! I want to make Boba Fett!"

"Yes, but C-3PO and R2-D2 get to hang out together a lot," said Amy, giving Lance a big smile. He smiled back and took the paper, and the rest of us all barfed.

FUTURE
MACE
WINDU

Then Dwight pulled out a brown sheet and gave it to me. "Here, Mike. Mace Windu protects the Holocron Keeper," he said. "And here's some purple for his lightsaber."

PURPLE

"SWEET!" I said. Mace Windu = AWESOME!

"Why Mike? Shouldn't I be Mace Windu?" asked Kellen.

"Yeah, and shouldn't I be the Holocron Keeper?" said Tommy.

"NO!" I said. "I'M Mace Windu AND the Holocron Keeper!"

MIKE

"Worry not, Kellen . . . Luke Skyfolder you will make," Origami Yoda told him.

"Oh . . . okay, well, I can't say no to Luke!" said Kellen. "He's mega-stooky!"

FUTURE
LUKE

"What about me?" asked Tommy.

"Stop interrupting you must!" said Origami Yoda.

"Sara, you should keep Chewie and Han," said Dwight. "And Rhondella, you can be Ahsoka. Here's some paper for you."

The paper was kind of orange on one side and white with blue stripes on the other. I guess that was to make her head-tentacle things, or whatever those are.

FUTURE AHSOKA

Rhondella just looked at it and said, "A-what-a?"

"Ahsoka," said Lance. "You know, Anakin's Padawan from *The Clone Wars*. She's massively bolt!"

AHSOKA

"Uh," said Rhondella, "no thanks. I didn't realize we were going to sit around here playing with paper dolls. I think I'll go see how Jen is doing. We need to talk about yearbook stuff anyway." And she got up and left.

"IF I join . . . and it's still an IF," said Harvey, "I get to be Anakin."

RHONDELLA

"Of course," said Dwight, handing him a sheet that was black and white.

"No thanks, dude," said Harvey. "I'm prepared." He held up his old Darth Paper and flipped the helmet back to show the face underneath.

"Captain Dwight . . . meet Anakin Skyfolder."

"Nice folding!" said Dwight. "So, are you joining?"

"This battle is inevitable," said Anakin.

"Yes, but . . . ARE. YOU. JOINING?" said Sara.

"Yeah, well . . . probably, but you guys haven't asked the important question yet: What do we do when Rabbski finds out?"

"Oh . . . find out she must . . . ," said Origami Yoda. "Only if–she knows can we win."

"Huh?" said Harvey.

"Aha!" said Amy. "I get it. It's not really about failing the tests. It's about SAYING we will fail the tests. Hopefully, she will be so scared by us saying we'll fail the tests that she will fix things and then we won't actually have to do it."

"You think SHE will be scared by US?" said Quavondo. "More like the other way around!"

"I didn't mean she would actually be frightened," said Amy. "But I think if we get enough rebels and show her some numbers, then she will have to do something."

"Yee-ha! Math power! You show her, kid!" said Han Foldo.

"Uh-huh," said Quavondo. "I'm still trying to figure out WHO is going to go march up to Ms. Rabbski and show her all this."

"That job will go to our leader . . . ," said Dwight, handing Tommy a sheet of paper that was brown on one side and white on the other. "Foldy-Wan Kenobi."

Harvey's Comment

I'm still not clear . . . is Tommy our leader, or is it foldy-wan? Either way, I need to borrow Lance's c-3Po to say, "we're doomed!"

My Comment: Thanks for the support, Padawan! You do realize that you're my Padawan now, right, Padawan?

Actually, I'm a little uncomfortable about being Obi-Wan. I thought I was going to write a case file about this rebellion, not be out front waving a lightsaber around! And I sure don't want to be the one to face Ms. Rabbski! She is going to EXPLODE!

Sara's Comment

> I'M NOT SURE IF EITHER OF YOU NOTICED, BUT RHONDELLA DIDN'T COME BACK . . .

Kellen's Comment

> I NOTICED

SCIENTIFIC EVIDENCE

BY HARVEY

okay, all that other stuff is fine, but I'm planning to present Rabbski with some scientific evidence. And I'll get a science fair project out of it, too!

Hypothesis: FunTime actually has a negative effect on my brain.

Method: Every night I will play the app BrainBusters2Life and record my score. Even though the app has math problems similar to those in our school tests, I expect my score to decline as FunTime makes me dumber by muddying the crystal-clear workings of my brain with stupid songs and cartoons.

control: My cousin JC is also going to be playing BrainBusters2Lite. Although his score will probably be much lower than mine, it should hold steady or even improve, since he is not being subjected to FunTime at his school.

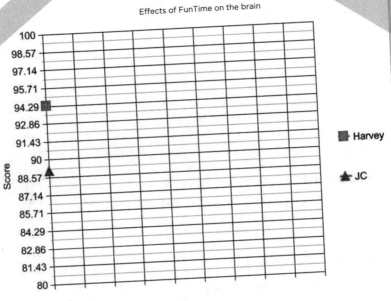

Effects of FunTime on the brain

Day 1

Harvey: 94.3%

JC: 89.1%

[Note: My all-time high score is 98.3, so you can see that after just ONE DAY FunTime has already made me dumber!]

THE NUMBERS

BY AMY

So . . . Captain Dwight asked me to try to do some math to figure out how many people we need to join the rebellion. But he said I should fold Origami R2-D2 first. He told me to use some instructions he and Kellen had made, where the silver part of the paper makes his dome and the white part makes his body and legs.

When I got home, I tried it, using some regular scrap paper until I figured it out. Then I made it with the silver paper and used a Sharpie to draw on his "eyes" and "arms," or whatever you call those cameras and doodads he has.

PRACTICE ⟵

⟶ PERFECT!

I propped him up on the desk in my room and got ready to crunch some numbers. First I had to go to the state Department of Education website to get some data.

Augusta	North River MS	955/1	71/71/71	76	79	82
Augusta	S. Stewart MS	955/2	71/71/71	75	73	80
Augusta	West Arnst MS	955/3	71/71/71	73	74	80
Augusta	Finkelville MS	955/4	71/71/71	69*	71	72

* denotes a score that fails to meet minimum accreditation benchmark

PROF GAP (Finkelville -2) -- Conditionally Accredited
>>>>>>>>>>>>>>>>>>>>>>>

All Students Division 84 100 0 84 100 0 66 99 1D
>>LucasCO>>Middle>>All

District	School	B6-AMO	BNCHMRK	CrV:ENG	CrV:MTH	CrV:SOC
Lucas Co.	StewartsvilleMS	964/1	70/70/70	82	83	80
Lucas Co.	T.R. Federle MS	964/2	69/69/69	76	81	81
Lucas Co.	Vinton MS	964/3	69/69/<	77	83	73
Lucas Co.	Kravtin Heights MS	964/4	68/68/68	67*	75	73
Lucas Co.	R. McQuarrie MS	964/000	68/68/68	71	65*	64*

* denotes a score that fails to meet minimum accreditation benchmark

PROF GAP (Kravtin -1) -- Conditionally Accredited
PROF GAP (McQuarrie -3/-4) --Non-Accredited -- ProfG1000-987a-7 on file

OUTRAGE!

>>>>>>>>>>>
All Students Division 83 100 0 83 100 0 43 99 1F
>>LockwoodCO>>Middle>>All

District	School	B6-AMO	BNCHMRK	CrV:ENG	CrV:MTH	CrV:SOC
Lockwood Co.	J. Wells MS	972/1	69/69/69	77	81	79
Lockwood Co.	D. Filoni MS	972/2	69/69/69	72	78	74

Here's what I learned about the Standards of Learning test. The possible scores are from 0 to 100. Each student has to get at least a 68 to pass. And the average of all students in each grade has to be 68 for the school to pass.

Last year McQuarrie Middle School students failed two of the three state Standards of Learning tests that middle-schoolers have to take: Average sixth-grade English score was 71. Average seventh-grade math score was 65. Average eighth-grade social studies score was 64.

You see what's outrageous here, right? Last year we were in the SIXTH GRADE!!! We passed our test! But because the kids who were in the seventh and eighth grade last year failed their tests, all of a sudden we have to have FunTime and do a billion boring worksheets. This is a total injustice!

I don't really blame those kids who failed, though. The tests are really weird. I mean, I paid attention in class and tried to study the important stuff, but then when I got in there to take the test, it seemed like it was full of all the UNimportant stuff.

I only passed by a few points and my parents gave

me a big lecture when I got my scores back.

But anyway, on to the math . . .

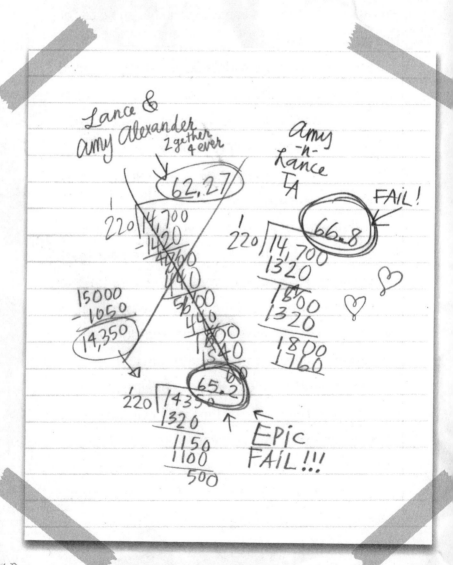

To pass the math test, we seventh-graders need to raise the average score by 3 points.

Let's say that FunTime works and we do even better. The new average might be 70. (Plus, 70 is easier for me to multiply than 68!)

There are 220 kids in the seventh grade this year.

So 70 x 220 = 15,400 total points.

BUT each kid who joins the rebellion is going to bring that average down. Instead of a 70 (or better), they'll get a 0.

So if ten kids do it, that's 700 points.

15,400 − 700 = 14,700

And that would make the new average . . . 14,700 ÷ 220 = 66.8. Even if you round up, that's 67 points. And 67 points = FAIL!

We might want to be more careful than that, though. If we got fifteen kids, that would make the average . . . 15,400 − 1,050 = 14,350. 14,350 ÷ 220 = 65.2.

McQuarrie scored 65 on the test last year! So not only would we fail, but we would make it look like FunTime hadn't done a thing!

So, my suggestion—and R2-D2 agrees—is that we need fifteen kids from each grade to join the rebellion!

Harvey's Comment

Wow, I like this. Actual facts and figures for once. Of course, you're forgetting that some people do a lot better than 70 on these tests. I got a 98 last year. So if I go down to 0, I'll have a much greater effect on the average than, say ... Tommy or Kellen.

My Comment: Gee, thanks. I can totally see why Captain Dwight let you be Anakin.

MURKY + PAD·MÉ

QUEEN ORIGAMIDALA AND THE BREAK-DANCING DICTIONARY

BY MURKY

heard about the rebellion

IM IN!

Got Dwight to help me make Queen Origamidala

also known as Pad-mé (like pad of paper)

Me: What do you think about funtime, Pad-mé?

Queen Origamidala: So this is how liberty
dies . . . with a break-dancing dictionary

yeah thats right a break-dancing dictionary!!!!!!!!!!!!!!!!!!!!!!!!!!!!

I guess you seventh-graders may not know

MOONWALK

about what our sixth-grade funtime videos are like. Ya, ya, Im sure your singing calculator is mega-spugly but what we have to watch is worse times a jillion!

since the sixth-grade test is on english and grammar and stuff Professor FunTime sings pikpok songs about commas or whatever and then he shouts: "Show 'em what I mean Wordsworth"

no matter what Professor FunTime has been narnaring on about Wordsworth the Break-dancing Dictionary does the exact same dance! the show is so cheap they only paid for one dance animation!!!!! not that anyone really wants to see MORE dances or anything but it is ridiculous that we have to watch him do the same thing over and over and over

first he moonwalks onto the screen then he flips over and does a headspin and while hes spinning words fly out of his pages spin around the screen and then form a sentence

HEADSPIN

since the show is total absolute narnar i
have been spending my time trying to invent
a word that is epically awful enough to be
worthy of Wordsworth. see the people at
our school only have two words to describe
things: awesome and sucks. well they use
sucks about a thousand times a day for
every little thing that isnt completely
perfect so then when they find something
that is much much much worse the best they
can do is "really sucks"

no

not good enough

or actually not BAD enough!

Heres what I got:

Chugbutt, tanning salon, mothra-meat,
rhinestone gravy, corpuscle, pikpokology,
slypate thursday, brickbat, non-shinky,
un-phred, foot, smorefoot

one word I came up with was infomercial
and then i realized thats pretty much what
funtime is like just without the 1-800

RHINESTONE GRAVY ON
MOTHRA-MEAT. MMM!

number and the shipping and handling charges

failstorm 9000, cud-flavored yogurt fish, snormlik, groutly, instabarf, backmarnette, guttersock, doglickspot

but then i started to realize that i was thinking too hard. if theres one thing i should know its that you cant force a word its got to come naturally like stooky did

HEY LANCE!

HEY STOOKY!

one day i was just walking up to say hey Lance and instead i said hey stooky and a new word was born and people kept asking me what it meant or if it was a noun or an adjective and stuff like that but there are no answers there is only stooky

so i just stared at Wordsworth watching the words spin out wasting our time with every spin and i knew in my heart what the one and only word for it was:

NOSTRUL

And you can add extra s's as needed: nosssssssssstrul!

Harvey's Comment ←

First of all, what is the deal with Murky picking Queen Amidala as his puppet? Huh? I mean, nobody has picked Boba Fett yet! He could have been Boba or Bossk or somebody awesome, but ... Padmé?

So this is a chance for me to use this new word in a sentence: As always, Murky's behavior is TOTALLY nosssssssstrul.

My Comment: Don't fight the "nostrul," Harvey. Lance and Kellen have already started saying it. And it's definitely better than hearing people say "this sucks" all the time.

But what IS "nostrul"? Does it mean nostril? Did Murky just misspell "nostril"? Is it a noun? An adjective? Actually, I think it works pretty well as a verb: Professor FunTime really nostrulled today!

Whatever it is, we're stuck with it now!

By the way, the preceding chapter was basically Murky's way of saying he's part of the rebellion and is going to use his new word to recruit other sixth-graders to join us. And, while I was surprised that he picked Padmé for his puppet, she WAS awfully good at getting people to join her cause in the movie . . .

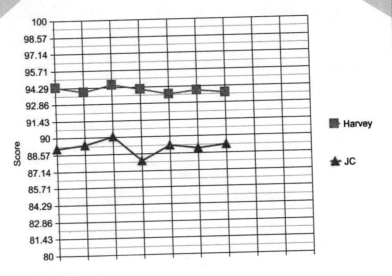

Effects of FunTime on the brain

Day 7

Harvey: 93.7%

JC: 89.3%

[Note: My scores are already slipping! When I try to concentrate, I see that stupid calculator!]

THE LETTER TO RABBSKI

BY TOMMY

Dwight helped me fold Foldy-Wan Kenobi. And he is awesome!

And as soon as I put him on my finger, I felt more courage! Like . . . yes, we can fight the FunTime Empire . . . and win!

But I didn't feel quite enough courage to actually go and tell Rabbski that in person . . . especially when it seemed so much easier to write her a letter and just let everybody sign it.

So Kellen, Harvey, and I wrote it last

...ER... UH...
..HERE'S
A... UH....
LETTER...

FOLDY-WAN
RABBSHI

night. And this morning we got everybody we could to sign it. Here it is . . .

Dear Principal Rabbski,

WE THE STUDENTS of McQuarrie Middle School . . . are bored out of our minds.

FunTime is terrible! It is the worst thing ever.

FunTime is killing our brains . . . so our brains are going on strike!

You are counting on all of us getting good scores on the state Standards tests to improve McQuarrie's average.

BUT . . .

UNLESS FUNTIME IS ENDED . . .

UNLESS ELECTIVES ARE RESTORED . . .

UNLESS OUR FIELD TRIP IS BACK ON . . .

We will purposefully FAIL our tests! That will make the average much lower!

We calculate that having fifteen students per grade join our rebellion will be enough to cause McQuarrie to FAIL the state Standards. We have sixteen seventh-graders, eight sixth-graders, and four eighth-graders so far. Each day that our fellow students must sit through the mind-rotting FunTime, more will join us.

Signed,

Tommy Lomax
SARA BOLT
KELLEN CAMPBELL
lance alexander
Amy Youmans
Mike Coley
+22 MORE!!!!!

MEETING WITH RABBSKI

BY MIKE, THE HOLOCRON KEEPER

We figured we would get called to the office so Rabbski could yell at us, so Kellen loaned me his recorder thingy so I wouldn't have to try to remember everything everybody said for the Holocron.

We were in sixth period when the PA called me, Tommy, Harvey, and Sara to the office. I don't know why Rabbski didn't call the rest. Well, I figure I do know why she didn't bother with Dwight. She's afraid of him and Origami Yoda! (Either that or she thought he'd just say "purple" over and over. Which is possible.)

Purple, Purple, Purple, Purple, Purple Pur

Dwight came anyway. We had to stand around in the office for about ten minutes before Rabbski opened her door and called us in.

"The Force will be with us," Tommy said, holding up Foldy-Wan Kenobi.

"Always," said Origami Yoda.

That's when I started the recording . . .

Rabbski: All right, everybody, sit down and . . . no, no, no . . . we're not doing puppets. Put those away

Tommy: We'd like to keep them out.

Rabbski: No. I said put them away, so you WILL put them away. See, I think you kids have forgotten who is in charge at this school. I am the one who makes the decisions.

Harvey: Well, if you decide that we have to put our origami away, then we won't listen.

Rabbski: Wheessshhh! [That's what it sounded like. I don't know how you spell it.] You kids have gotten a little

WHEESSSHHH!

bit   too   big   for   your   britches.
[None of us could answer that because we
had no idea what she was talking about.]
[Then she sat down and fiddled with the
Rubik's Cube on her desk. Then she took
a deep breath.]

4×4!

Rabbski: Look, this is serious business. You kids
are messing with something that is a very
big deal. The state takes these tests
seriously. So does the school board, and
so do I.

Tommy: So do we, Ms. Rabbski.

Rabbski: Then why are you willing to jeopardize
it all just because of those puppets?

Tommy: Why are you?

Rabbski: Tommy, you have turned into a real smart
aleck this year! Okay, fine, keep the
puppets. You're here to listen, anyway,
not talk. Now, are you listening?

About half of us: Yes, Ms. Rabbski.

Rabbski: I am very, very disappointed in all of
you. This is not the sort of—

Harvey: Well, we're disappointed in FunTime. It
             stinks!

Rabbski: Harvey! I said you were here to listen!
             No more out of you!

[More fiddling with the Rubik's Cube.]

Rabbski: In fact . . . you know what? Just forget
             it. I was going to try to treat you like
             adults and talk this through. But forget
             it. All you need to know is one thing:
             Students who fail the test may be held
             back a year, at the discretion of the
             principal.

Tommy: What does "at the discretion of the
             principal" mean?

Rabbski: It means this: If you flunk the test,
             I won't let you move on to the eighth
             grade. You'll stay in the seventh grade,
             watching the SAME FUNTIME program all
             over again until you pass. Fail the
             test, fail the grade. Simple, right?

[Silence.]

Rabbski: RIGHT! Now . . . who's ready to get

back on the McQuarrie Team and pass those tests with flying colors? All of you. Good. Now . . . you go back to class and this letter goes in the trash! What does your puppet have to say about that, Tommy?

Foldy-Wan Kenobi: Uh . . .

Rabbski: I think the words you were looking for were "Yes, Principal Rabbski," but at least we're making progress.

Harvey's Comment

"UH"???? That's what Foldy-WAD Kenobi had to say? "UH"? The Hero of the Clone Wars. The Jedi Knight who beat Darth Maul. The man who faced Darth Vader UNAFRAID says, "Uh..."?

Well, this is just great!

My Comment: I guess I was hoping Foldy-Wan would know what to say. Because I sure didn't.

DEFEAT

BY TOMMY

We all slunk out of Rabbski's office.

"Well, that didn't last long," said Harvey.

"Yeah, sorry, Dwight, but there is no way I am going to fail seventh grade," Mike said. "My mom would freak."

"Yeah, mine, too!" said Kellen. "And what if I had Mr. Howell for FunTime again all next year?"

"It was a neat idea, though, Dwight," I said, trying to cheer us both up. "I mean, it was good advice from Origami Yoda."

"Give up so easily do you?" croaked Origami Yoda.

"Uh, yeah," said Sara. "I mean, FunTime stinks, but failing a grade is like . . ."

"WUG!" said Chewbacca.

"Yeah, man, it's wug," said Kellen. "Very, very wug!"

We all started to go.

"Wait!" said Origami Yoda. "The Origami Rebel Alliance . . . meet again we must."

"What for, Dwight? We can't do thi—"

"MUST!" shouted Origami Yoda. "Tonight."

"Tonight?" I said. "You don't mean at—"

"Fun Night!"

"Ugh, no . . . ," said just about everybody.

Fun Night is not actually part of FunTime . . . but they are similar in the way that getting eaten by a reek and getting eaten by a Sarlacc are similar. Fun Night is what they call our monthly school dances.

Actually, once—thanks to Origami Yoda—we did have actual fun on Fun Night. But only

once. And after that we had all just sort of agreed to stop going. We knew it would never be that much fun again . . . In fact, it could be a disaster. It felt like we had beaten Fun Night, and nobody wanted to risk a rematch.

"Sorry, Dwight, we're kinda done with those," said Sara.

"Then choose you must. Fun Night . . . or FunTime!"

"But, Dwight, what are we going to talk about? I mean . . . we just lost," I said. "That was like Order 66, when the clone troopers shot all the Jedi in the back! This whole 'rebellion' just got crushed by the Empress!"

"No!" said Origami Yoda. "Search your feelings, Foldy-Wan . . ."

Well, this is kind of embarrassing, but when I searched my feelings, I thought it might actually be kind of fun to dance with Sara again. I mean, that one great Fun Night was almost a whole year ago. Maybe this was all some sort of plan Origami Yoda/Dwight had to get us both to Fun Night, and maybe he would have some special song play and we would dance, and maybe . . . Well, that's not important right now.

All that's important right now is that I held up Foldy-Wan and said, "Okay."

And of course, Harvey said, "'Okay'? Wow, more inspiring words from our leader! But I'll come because my mom is always pushing me to go, anyway."

"Did I say stand around in the hall?" It was Rabbski sticking her head out of the office. "No, I said, 'Go back to class!' NOW!"

We went, and in the end most of us agreed to go to Fun Night.

Harvey's Comment

Interesting that FunTime and Fun Night both have the word "fun" in them but they aren't fun. I wonder if the word "fun" is ever used for things that are actually fun. For instance, it's not Star

WONKA FUNDIP = ACTUALLY FUN!

Fun Wars or LEGO Fun Bricks or captain Funderpants or Funcraft!

My Comment: Funcraft? Oh . . . Minecraft + fun, right. Actually, I kind of like the sound of Captain Funderpants! I would definitely read that!

I'm still hoping to disprove Harvey's argument by thinking of something fun that has "fun" in the name . . . but I haven't thought of it yet.

Lords and Ladies!!! It's time for Ye Olde McQuarrie Middle School's

FUN KNIGHT!

Where: Music in the cafeteria. Basketball in the gym
When: Friday @ 7   Cost: $3 or 1 canned food item

FRIDAY NIGHT JEDI COUNCIL MEETING AT FUN NIGHT

BY MIKE, THE HOLOCRON KEEPER

Site: Cafeteria stage

Attendance: Mike, Tommy, Kellen, Sara, Amy, Remi (sixth-grader), Murky (sixth-grader), Lance, Quavondo, Harvey, Dwight, James Suervo (eighth-grader)

Lance: James! What are you doing here?

James: I have to come now because of my brother. He's in the sixth grade, and he loves Fun Nights. So my parents make me come, too, so that they can go out to Applebee's alone.

HEY BABY!

JAMES'S BROTHER

Lance: That's painful! Listen, uh, we're going
to have a secret meeting here . . .
It's sort of like an Anti-FunTime club.

James: Anti-FunTime? I'm in!

Lance: You might get in trouble with Rabbski.

James: What does Origami Yoda say about it?

Lance: He's the one who started it.

James: Then I'm totally in!

Harvey: Isn't it a little loud for this meeting?
This crappy music is driving me nuts.

Captain Dwight: It will keep spies from over-
hearing us.

Harvey: Spies? Seriously?

Captain Dwight: Look at the snack bar.

[Principal Rabbski and Mr. Howell were standing
at the snack bar. She was talking to him while
glaring at us.]

Lance/C-3PO: What are they doing here in Cloud
City? We'll be destroyed for sure!

Captain Dwight: No! This way we can have the
meeting right under their noses. If
she comes close enough to hear, we

will change the subject to *Sesame
Street.*

Harvey: *Sesame Street?*

Captain Dwight: It's especially good this season.

Sara: Okay, listen. Can we get to the point? The point is I'm not going to be part of this anymore. There's just no way I'm going to risk failing seventh grade for this.

Origami Yoda: Says so does the brave and mighty Fortune Wookiee?

Sara: [Exasperated sigh.] Dwight, I hate to break it to you, but I was making up all that Fortune Wookiee stuff.

Origami Yoda: Were you? Were . . . you?

Harvey: I used to think FunTime was the worst thing in the universe, but now there's something new: this conversation.

Amy: Dwight, should I tell them my latest calculations?

Dwight: It's Captain Dwight . . . and yes.

Amy: [Gets out Origami R2-D2 and paper

covered in math scrawl.] Okay, guys, here's what Origami Yoda told me and R2 to figure out . . . and it works! We don't need to fail the tests! We just need to do worse.

Everybody: Huh? What? Worse? Huh?

Amy: Okay, remember how the best score is 100 and the score you need to pass is a 68. Well, we told Rabbski we would get 0, but everybody normally tries to get a 100. I mean, you would normally try to fill out all the right answers, right? But what if you didn't? What if you tried to get a 68?

Sara: Huh?

Amy: You only answer questions you're certain of. Once you get 68, or maybe 70 to be safe, you just stop and don't answer any more.

Sara: Nope, I still don't get it.

Harvey: I do! It actually makes sense. If, instead of my usual 95 or so, I got

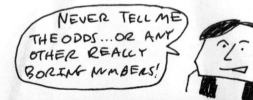

NEVER TELL ME THE ODDS...OR ANY OTHER REALLY BORING NUMBERS!

a 68, that would make a dent in the school-wide average.

DENT

Quavondo: A small dent.

SMALL DENTS

Amy: Yes, and just like before, what we need is a lot of small dents.

SMALLER SMALL DENTS

Quavondo: But these are smaller small dents. We'd be dropping our scores by 10 or 20 points, not 80 or 90 points. You would need a LOT more small dents.

Tommy: How many?

Amy: My calculations show that if forty students each dropped their scores by 15 points, and twenty dropped by 20, it should be enough.

Quavondo: Sixty students, total?

Amy: Er . . . it would be sixty per grade.

Everybody: PER GRADE?????

Origami Yoda: Yes . . . the Rebel Alliance must become a Rebel Army. Recruit more students we must.

Amy: We've got sixteen seventh-graders. So we need forty-four more.

Tommy: Forty-four more? Impossible!

Kellen/Luke: It's not impossible! I used to sign up womp rats back home and—

Amy: Ahem . . . can we focus? There's worse news: We've only got eight sixth-graders, so we need fifty-two more. Murky and Remi, can you guys help us?

Murky/Pad-mé: It is clear to me now that this middle school no longer functions. If we do not act quickly, all will be nostrul forever.

Me (Mike): Was that a yes?

Murky: Reeby, reeby!

Me: WOULD YOU JUST SAY YES OR NO???

Murky: Geez . . . yes.

Me: And you, Remi?

Remi's puppet: When a planet falls out of line, it must be corrected.

Me: Uh . . . who is that?

Remi: THIS is Mara Jade! Before she married Luke Skywalker!

Kellen: What? Luke doesn't get married!

Remi: In the comic books he does! Want me to loan you some? Maybe we could get together and—

Kellen: Uh . . . I guess right now we need to know if you and, uh, Mara are joining the rebellion or not.

Remi/Mara: Yes! Rabbski must prepare to face the unrelenting power of the sixth grade!

Harvey: 'Unrelenting power of the sixth grade'? All you guys do is giggle and whine.

Tommy: Uh, Harvey . . . we're trying to get them to JOIN us.

Captain Dwight: And as far as the eighth grade, what do you think, James?

Lance: Uh, James, dude, would you quit drawing on your hand and pay attention?

James Suervo: [He has drawn eyes and a mustache on the side of his hand and is moving the thumb upside down like a mouth.] You can call me Hando Calrissian . . . and I'm still in!

Amy: We've got four eighth-graders, and if you join that makes five. Can you find fifty-five more eighth-graders who hate FunTime? Especially ones who got high scores last time?

James/Hando: Anything for you, lovely math lady.

Lance: HEY!

James: Relax, dude! It was Hando talking, not me!

NO KIT FISTO!

Quavondo: I didn't bring my Kit Fisto puppet, but I'm sure he would say he doesn't think it's going to be so easy to talk kids into doing this. I'm not even sure if I'll do it. I mean, it's taking a big risk. What if you try to get a 68 and end up getting a 67. You fail and Rabbski destroys you!

Remi/Mara: Yeah, the risk is big, but remember: If we do nothing, we definitely lose! I don't know how bad your FunTime videos are, but ours are so bad it's turning us into zombies! I don't just mean

BRRAINNNNS!

we're bored—I mean we are about to start actually eating one another's brains!!

Kellen: Yeah, and don't forget art class and chorus, band, LEGOs, rockets, and all that stuff.

Lance: And don't forget the field trip! Last year we went to the zoo—

Quavondo: Don't remind me!

Lance: —and this year we're MAYBE going to Craphole Plantation??? Dude, it's, like, two blocks from my house! That's not a field trip!

Sara: Dwight was right. The Fortune Wookiee does want to do this! I mean, Han and Chewie would go for it.

Harvey: And so would Anakin! Totally! I'm in!

Murky/Pad-mé: Oh, Anakin, you're so brave. Hold me like you did on Naboo back before there were singing calculators and break-dancing dictionaries!

Harvey: Would you get that thing out of my

face? Geez, I still don't know what Anakin ever saw in her!

Captain Dwight: That just leaves our leader . . . Foldy-Wan, what do you say?

Tommy/Foldy-Wan: Uh . . . you know, it sounds great!

Harvey: Wow! What an inspiration you are, Tommy! Geez, if you don't know the movies, could you at least look up a few Obi-Wan quotes on Wookieepedia, please?

Remi: Hey, Mara has something to say.

Mara Jade: This needs to be a stealth mission. We can't let Rabbski know what we're doing until we've got the troops to back us up. On Monday, we come back. We go to class. We go to FunTime . . . but all the while we're working to undermine the system and quietly get more students to join us.

Kellen/Luke: Yeah! Then, once we have the numbers we need . . . commence attack on the Death Star!

Sara: This is it folks, we are REALLY rebels
           this time.

Origami Yoda:  May the Force be with us . . .

Harvey's Comment

I can't believe I'm saying this, but this plan is actually
awesome! But it's going to take brains. You're going
to have to be SURE you get 68 points, maybe 70 or 72
to be safe, and then you're going to have to be SURE
you're getting the rest of the questions wrong!
If you get any accidentally right, then you've
messed up!

   If we actually end up carrying out this threat,
it'll be easy for me, but the rest of you are really
going to have to be careful . . .

My Comment: Great . . . I love a plan that lets Harvey
brag more.

   But I do like the new plan! I just wish I could get
Foldy-Wan to say the right thing at the right time.
Maybe I WILL go on Wookieepedia and write down
some quotes.

There was something that happened after that meeting, by the way. It wasn't something good.

Remember how I thought maybe Dwight wanted us to go to Fun Night because he had some sort of plan involving me and Sara? Well, it was pretty obvious that that was the last thing on his mind.

But I figured . . . as long as we're both at Fun Night, I might as well ask her to dance.

"Uh," she said. "Maybe later. I've got to talk to somebody."

Well, I was disappointed, of course, but I figured she was going to talk to Rhondella—who, of course, didn't come to our meeting.

But then Kellen said something about Rhondella not even being there at all. So I started looking around . . .

And all the way on the other side of the cafeteria, I saw Sara and Tater Tot together. And then Kellen's mom came to pick us up before I saw her again!

And Foldy-Wan finally had something to say: "I've got a bad feeling about this."

SARA + FORTUNE WOOKIEE

OH, GOOD GRIEF . . .

BY SARA

Oh, good grief!

Here we go again with Tater Tot panic! ← OFFICIALLY KNOWN AS T.T.P.!

"Oh, no! Sara talked to Tater Tot. Better ask Origami Yoda what to do!!!!"

I'm perfectly capable of talking to Tater Tot for two minutes without falling in love with him. In fact, I sat next to him for the first half of the year in home ec and didn't even come close.

But he IS an okay guy. A little competitive. A little too interested in sports. But he's not evil or anything . . .

And I happen to know something about him that the rest of you guys don't.

. RESISTIBLE →

Last year, he got the highest score in the whole grade on the Standards of Learning test.

Yes, Harvey, I know you THINK you got the highest score on the test, but Tater Tot actually did. Don't ask me how he did it, but he did. And I know he did because he was bragging to me and I didn't believe him, so he showed me his result sheet. He got a 99!

He only missed one question!

People, I got an 88. Tater Tot is 11 points smarter than me . . . which is kind of scary!

So anyway . . . Amy said we needed to recruit people. Especially people who had really high scores last year.

So I went over to talk to him about it during Fun Night.

Apparently, he and a bunch of his basketball buddies were ready to revolt anyway. They hate FunTime, too, of course, but he said the real reason is that Ms. Toner told him they weren't going to have JV wrestling in the spring. Apparently, JV wrestling is the most important thing in the world, because I had to hear about it for fifteen minutes. And then Tater Tot called his friends over and we explained it all to them and that took

76

another fifteen minutes, and when I finally got back to the stage all of you guys were long gone!

But the important thing is I just got us eight more rebels. And probably more when Tater Tot tells some of the other JV types about it.

But he has two conditions . . .

First, we have to add JV wrestling and all other sports to our list of demands. Second, they want origami clone troopers. Dwight that's your department . . .

Harvey's Comment

I'm sorry, there is no way that Tater the Tott beat me on that Standards test. No way!

My Comment: Sorry, Sara!!! It's just scary to see you talking to Tater Tot since so many other girls think he's so awesome. And finding out that he's also supersmart doesn't help. And I still think he might be doing all this just to try to get another chance with you. But I'm sorry if I was a butt about it.

Effects of FunTime on the brain

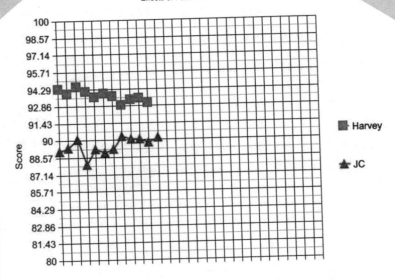

Day 12

Harvey: forgot!

JC: 90.2%

[Note: ARGHHH! forgot to play app because of that stupid fun Night!]

HARVEY, AND
ANAKIN/VADER

ORIGAMI ANAKIN AND THE P.E. TEACHER

BY LANCE

My note: This is Harvey's story, but he refuses to write it up. So I've asked Lance to write it up since he is in Harvey's P.E. class and was there.

Okay, what is it now? February, right? Well, Harvey has been whining in P.E. ever since school started … in August!

He whines about lots of things, of course, but the constant thing is when we do sit-ups. Last year, Ms. Toner had us do a few warm-up exercises, including sit-ups. The kind where you put your legs out straight and sit up and try to touch your toes.

LET'S HAVE FUN!

M S. TONER

MR. TOLEN

DON'T MESS AROUND!

Well, this year, we've got Mr. Tolen for P.E. And he's very serious about the warm-ups. No matter what we're doing, we have to stretch and warm up for ten minutes first. (One time we actually warmed up and then sat down on the floor with pencils and paper and took a test on rules, like the size of a basketball court. Why did we need to warm up to write?) Anyway, part of the warm-up is twenty-five sit-ups.

Mr. Tolen makes us do the kind where you bend your legs, put your hands behind your head, and then sit up and touch an elbow to a knee.

WHO CARES? you ask.

HARVEY CARES, I answer.

I CARE!

At the beginning of the year, he got in an argument with Mr. Tolen every day for the first two weeks. Mr. Tolen is the sort of teacher who yells back. So eventually Harvey stopped arguing directly with him.

Some days he tries to do straight-leg sit-ups, but that starts a fight with Tolen, too. So most of the time he does the bent-leg sit-ups and complains the whole time!

When we start doing warm-ups, Tolen puts on music (usually the worst music in the universe; right now it's

STRAIGHT LEG!

BENT LEG

PRESENTING:
MR TOLEN'S
800 YEAR
OLD CD PLAYER...

SOUNDS
LIKE
CRUD

that song called "Kiss This Kiss!"), but you can still hear Harvey over there griping. It sounds like this:

"My father's a biologist and . . ."

"Kiss me! Uh-huh, kiss me!"

". . . he says bent-knee sit-ups are an inefficient way to exercise and . . ."

"Kiss me when I'm kissing you!"

". . . may strain the back, and studies have shown that . . ."

"And I'll kiss you, too! OOH!"

And on and on . . .

Some days Tolen just ignores it. Some days he yells at Harvey. A couple of times he even sent Harvey to Rabbski's office.

Well . . . okay, that's the back story. Here's what happened this time:

Harvey didn't do the sit-ups. He just stood there while all the rest of us got on the floor and started doing them.

"What now, Harvey?" asked Mr. Tolen. "Do I need to send you to Ms. Rabbski again?"

"Go ahead! But you can't send all of us!" Harvey said.

"Why would I want to send all of you? You're the only one who complains."

Our gym shorts don't have pockets, so I don't know where he was hiding it, but ... Harvey suddenly held up Anakin Skyfolder! I couldn't believe it! Harvey always says Dwight is embarrassing when he has Origami Yoda out at lunch or whatever ... but a finger puppet in P.E.???? Now THAT is embarrassing!

"You underestimate our power!" said Anakin. "This ends now!"

"Actually, it ends on twenty-five," said Mr. Tolen. "So you better get started."

"No!" said Anakin. "I won't. And I'm not alone!"

Then Harvey turned around and looked at the rest of us!

"Lance! Mike! Cassie! Dwight! We can stop this, too. Just like with the tests. We just have to stand together."

I was totally, totally embarrassed. I mean, I'm a guy who has done a tap dance routine in the library ... but this was more embarrassing. Everybody was looking at me like they expected me to jump up and wave C-3PO and join him. I didn't have C-3PO with me, but I knew what he would have said about Harvey's behavior: "HOW RUDE!"

HOW RUDE!

So I just kept on doing sit-ups. I think I was way past twenty-five by that time.

"C'mon, guys! Stand up!" said Harvey. (We didn't.) "I thought you guys were rebels!"

I must have been up to fifty by that time, and I couldn't do anymore. I had to stop.

"Harvey ... nobody else wants to rebel against sit-ups," I said. "Nobody else cares."

"But they're bad sit-ups! Studies show that ..."

"ENOUGH!" shouted Mr. Tolen. "Harvey, go on down to Ms. Rabbski's office."

That's when Harvey/Anakin lost it!

"This is outrageous! This is unfair!" Anakin started yelling. And then Harvey yelled, "If the rest of you would just stand up with me, we could stop this. If none of us do the sit-ups, Tolen will have to change!"

"Harvey, I said ENOUGH!" said Mr. Tolen, and he started stomping toward Harvey.

Harvey must have been really, really desperate, because he actually spoke to Origami Yoda!

"Origami Yoda! Tell them to join me! Tell Dwight to join me!"

HELP ME ORIGAMI YODA! YOU'RE MY ONLY HOPE!

Mr. Tolen had just about reached Harvey by then, and I wasn't sure what he was going to do . . . wrestle him to the ground or something?

But suddenly, a screechy voice rang out in the gym and Mr. Tolen stopped. Harvey stopped. We all stopped and looked at Dwight.

He had Origami Yoda. (Again, I don't know where he got it from . . .)

And Origami Yoda said, "No, Anakin. Mistaken you are. Sit-up style matters not. Warming up matters not. About more than these phys ed is."

Harvey: "Huh?"

Origami Yoda: "Discipline is what Tolen teaches us. Obedience must you learn, Padawan . . ."

I expected Harvey to really, really lose it after that. And for a second it really looked like he was going to.

Then Anakin said, "Sometimes we must do what is requested of us."

And Harvey just dropped to the ground and started doing sit-ups. Twenty-five bent-leg sit-ups!

Mr. Tolen just stood there. A minute earlier he had looked like the Incredible Hulk, and now he didn't have anybody to stomp on. Then he just laughed.

"Dwight, I think you've got P.E. all figured out," he said.

"Purple," said Dwight.

Harvey's Comment

No comment.

My Comment: Actually, that does make all the horrors of P.E. make a little more sense. The basketball drills. The shuttle run. Folk dances. Running laps around the gym. Chin-ups. Hoccer! It's kind of like when Yoda made Luke run around the swamp and eat root stew and do headstands and all that. Luke didn't really need to learn to do headstands; he had to learn discipline, obedience, focus, all that kind of stuff.

Could P.E. actually be training us to be Jedi? If so, I'm in big trouble, since I got a B- for the last six weeks.

DWIGHT QUITS!

CAPTAIN DWIGHT QUITS THE REBELLION (BRIEFLY)

BY TOMMY

A lot of the files in these case files seem to happen in the cafeteria. This one actually starts in the lunch line where they hand you your tray.

The lunch lady who takes our lunch tickets handed us a slip of paper.

At the top of it, it said: HEALTHYUMS.

"Does this say 'Health Yums' or 'Healthy Ums'?" Harvey asked her.

"Don't know. That's just what it says on all the boxes they loaded into the big freezer this morning."

"What are they?"

"Oh, just something new for you kids to complain about, probably."

That would of course turn out to be correct. The new food was nasty. Like, they replaced the chicken nuggets (which had been only half nasty) with this stuff that sort of looked like a piece of grilled chicken. And it even tasted a little like grilled chicken. But it didn't chew like chicken. It chewed like one of those cushion things in your shoes.

½ NASTY

ALL NASTY!

And suddenly there wasn't chocolate milk anymore. And the popsicle line started selling just one kind of popsicle and no matter which flavor you got—cherry, grape, root beer, etc.—the main ingredients were water and apple juice.

But all that is stuff we found out later. That first day all we knew was what it said on the HealthYum slip. When we got to the table, we sat down and read the whole thing:

DUDE! THIS TOTALLY TASTES LIKE APPLE!

MINE, TOO! WAH!

Dear Students and Parents,

We've always served balanced, nutritious meals in our cafeteria, but a number of parents have raised concerns about the levels of artificial colors, preservatives, and high-fructose corn syrup that were present.

Your concerns are our concerns . . . and so we are proud to announce some big changes as we switch to the HealthYum family of foods—a new catalog of delicious and healthy choices from our food service provider, Edu-Fun.

These have been specially formulated to offer great taste while cutting back on the preservatives and syrups. And they completely eliminate trans fats.

For instance, the fatty and heavily colored Rib-B-Q sandwich will be replaced with HealthYums' FarmFresh™ HunnyHam Sandwich.

We'll still be serving your children delicious meals, but now you can rest assured that they're Healthy as well as Yummy!

"STILL"?
WHEN DID
THEY START?

MWAHAHA!!!

Laura Mihalick
Dietician and Nutritionist
Lucas County School District

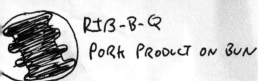

RIB-B-Q
PORK PRODUCT ON BUN

HUNNY-HAM
PORK PRODUCT ON BUN

"Oh, Jabba! Wait until Dwight hears about this," Harvey said, laughing. "No more Rib-B-Q!"

"It's *Captain* Dwight," said Captain Dwight, who had just walked up with his own tray and slip. "What about the Rib-B-Q?"

"It's gone, dude!"

"Today's not Rib-B-Q day. That's going to be on Friday."

"No, it's not!" brayed Harvey. He held up Anakin and flipped his Darth Paper helmet back on.

"They are altering the menu," said Darth Paper. "They will never again serve . . . the Rib-B-Q."

I didn't really want to get involved, but I couldn't stand to see Harvey mess around with Dwight anymore . . .

"Yeah, look, dude. They're replacing it with a ham sandwich." And I showed him where it said it on the slip of paper.

I expected him to go crazy. To flip out and

stand on his seat or run around screaming.
(These are all things he does fairly often,
after all.)

Instead, he looked at me and said, "Lock
S-foils in attack position."

"Huh?"

"It's time to write our new letter to
Rabbski. To let her know we have almost forty
students who want their classes, their field
trip, their sports, and their Rib-B-Qs back."

"Uh, Dwight, I'm sorry to say this, but I
think you're the only person who ever ate the
Rib-B-Q. Everybody else is glad to see it go."

"This will be a day long remembered. It
has seen the end of the Rib-B-Q, and soon—"
started Darth Paper, but Kellen and I told
Harvey to shut up.

"But we can still demand—" started Dwight.

"No, we can't!" said Kellen. "We can't add
a bunch of crazy stuff to our list or she'll
never take us seriously."

"It's true," said Sara.

THE
RIB-ELLION!

"It's not crazy—it's Rib-B-Q!" yelled Dwight.

"I'm sorry, Dwight," I said. "I mean . . . listen, everybody, is there anyone here who wants to make the Rib-B-Q part of the rebellion?"

Everyone giggled or laughed or snorted or said, "Sorry, Dwight."

Dwight said, "Purple!"

I got out Foldy-Wan, who said, "Search your feelings, Dwight. You know the Rib-B-Q isn't worth rebelling over."

"Fine, then I'm dropping out of the rebellion!"

"WHAT????" said me and Kellen and Lance and Mike and Sara.

"C'mon, Captain Dwight—"

"No, it's just Dwight again," he said, and took off his cape.

"Well, things are looking up already," said Harvey. "Foldy-Wad has finally done something right—he got Dwight to quit!"

"Will you shut it, Harvey?!?" I said. Then: "Uh, Dwight? You're not really quitting, are you?"

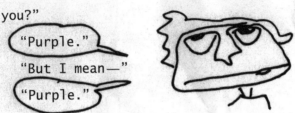

"Purple."

"But I mean—"

"Purple."

"But how are we supposed to do the rebellion without Origami Yoda?"

"Pur—" started Dwight, but then his arm shot up in the air. Yoda was on his finger.

"Still part of the rebellion am I," said Origami Yoda.

"But not Dwight?" I asked.

"Hrmmm, no, not Dwight . . . Choose his own path he must."

"Oh, good," said Harvey. "For a little while there I was worried that Dwight wasn't a complete lunatic anymore. But he is, so—"

"But, Origami Yoda, can't you give Dwight some advice to help him choose the right path?" I asked.

"Matter not it will . . . The Force his

ally is. It connects all things . . . even Dwight and Rib-B-Qs . . ."

Just then, Lunchman Jeff showed up carrying a big white box with some oven mitts.

"Psst, Dwight, check this . . ."

The box was covered in frost. Lunchman Jeff rubbed some of it off with a mitt.

144 RIB-B-Q PATTIES, it said.

"They were going to throw these out," said Lunchman Jeff, "but I nabbed them for you. Your mom got a big freezer at home?"

Dwight nodded.

"All right, dude, then stop by after school and grab 'em. A hundred and forty-four, man. You can eat two a week for a year and still have some left over."

Dwight hugged Lunchman Jeff. (And Dwight never hugs anybody!) Then, when LJ left, Dwight put his cape back on.

And the rebellion was saved!

→ **or more likely, he will eat 144 a week for one week.**

My Comment: Geez, I hope not! That would kill a gundark!

Anyway, I'm glad Origami Yoda was there to save the day. You do have to wonder how Origami Yoda could have known help was coming when Dwight clearly didn't. But I promised Harvey I wouldn't make this case file about whether Origami Yoda is real or not. (Also, there is now SO MUCH evidence that he is real that there's hardly any point in wondering about it anyway! You'll notice that even Harvey rarely argues about it anymore . . . You've just got to accept it and deal with it.)

THE 144 RIB-B-Q MEAL!

LOOK AT THE SIZE OF THAT THING!

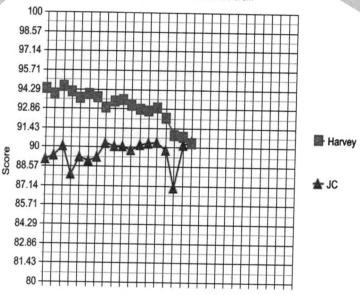

Effects of FunTime on the brain

Day 18: Harvey: 90.3%, JC: 90.5%

[Note: Oh. My. Jabba! It's worse than I thought! I'm already as dumb as my cousin! If this keeps on going, I could end up as dumb as . . . Tommy and Kellen! Oh, no!!! Save me! Save me!]

My note: Good grief!

Harvey may or may not be getting dumber, but he's definitely not getting any nicer!

Meanwhile, the rebellion continues to spread . . . even to the sixth grade! It's The Revenge of the Sixth . . .

ORIGAMI EWOK ATTACK!!!!!!!!!!

BY REMI

okay so if you want to know what the number-one problem we have over on the sixth-grade side of the building is its these three girls Brenna Lilly and Ciarra (honestly i dont know if i spelled that right or not, but i do know it starts with a c even though it sounds like an s).

anyway they are such a big problem that i dont think people even think of them as a problem anymore at least not a problem that can be changed . . . they are sort of like getting stuck in traffic on that road at the mall. you just get stuck there

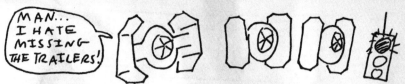

THE BLC

so much you dont even think that maybe some smart road person could fix it. you just think you are always going to get stuck and thats the way it is.

at least with the mall you know where youre going to get stuck—at the light in front of the theater (and get there late and miss all the good trailers)—but with the BLC (thats Brenna Lilly and Ciarra) you never know where youre going to get stuck.

in case youve never been over to the sixth-grade hall the reason you get stuck behind the BLC is that they walk down the hall with their arms around each other . . . its like theyre all three in love with how great they are so much that they cant let go and have to be a constant moving hug all the time.

a) this is obnoxious.

b) if you are coming the other way you have to go around them because they will never ever ever ever unlink their arms.

c) if you are behind them forget about

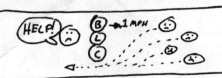

going around them because on each
side of them there is a steady stream
of people from (b) going around.

Kellen if you could draw pictures of this it would
help! Your pictures are the best part of any case
file anyway!!!!!

i think what bothers me the most is how smug
they are about it. they do it because they think
they are better than everyone and then everyone
moves out of their way and it makes them even more
sure that they are better so they do it again and
on and on and on . . .

WATERY

SLUDGY

okay so i was going to the library before school
to ask Dwight to ask Origami Yoda a question. it
wasnt about the rebellion it was just a normal
question. in fact the question was how can i get
my hot chocolate to stir up better. i always get a
watery drink and then end up with chocolate sludge
at the bottom.

so i was going to ask OY about this but I COULDNT
GET TO THE LIBRARY! i was stuck behind the BLC for
the gamillionth time.

Noooo!

and then suddenly it hit me . . . maybe OY could stop the BLC.

why had i never thought about this before? well like i said everybody seems to think the BLC is just a fact of life not something that can be changed. but i finally realized if Yoda can lift an x-wing out of a swamp maybe he can lift the BLC out of my way.

then the bell rang before i got to the library!!!!!!!! i told you that the BLC is a pain in the drain!

but i finally got to talk to Dwight after school waiting in the bus line since his bus line is next to my bus line.

i explained the situation.

YODA'S ARM

Origami Yoda: why go around them people do? why not go through? or make them around you go?

Me: because if you dont move out of their way they look at you like you are totally the dumbest lowest thing they've ever seen or maybe even make fun of you.

Origami Yoda: what so?

Me: what do you mean "so what"? how would

you like it if the three most popular
girls in the sixth grade made fun of you
in front of everybody?

Dwight: happens to me all the time. also seventh-
and eighth-grade girls . . . and sometimes
fourth- and fifth-grade girls on the bus . . .
and sometimes—

Me: yeah but youre . . .

Dwight: im CAPTAIN Dwight!

Me: uh, yeah, i know . . .

Origami Yoda: maybe Captain Remi you should be . . .

Me: would i have to wear a cape?

Origami Yoda: no, finger puppet you need . . .

Me: ·ive got one! [and i pulled out my Mara
Jade finger puppet.]

Me: but i dont know what to do with her . . .
except maybe clobber them . . .

Origami Yoda: no! control her dark side Mara Jade
learned to . . . so must you . . . even
so, the right choice she is not for this
mission.

Me: what? but shes awesome! and . . . i

A Cap

sort of have another reason for wanting to have Mara Jade. you know because of—

Origami Yoda: yes. know all about that we do . . . but for this mission leave Mara and her temper behind you must . . . stop the BLC alone you cannot. gather a tribe you must . . . a tribe of ewoks.

Me: oh! i made an origami ewok once! it was so cute!

Origami Yoda: good . . . . good . . . eight more you must make . . . and eight more kids to use them find.

Me: use them to do what? hit the BLC on the head with coconuts like in the movie?

BONK

Origami Yoda: in the movie that is not!

Me: well, whatever . . . are we supposed to launch an ewok attack?

Origami Yoda: yes . . . but hit them on the head you must not. A clever ewok trap you must spring.

well it wasnt hard to find eight people who were sick of the BLC but it was hard to find eight people

who were sick of the BLC AND willing to wear an ewok finger puppet AND get involved in some sort of hallway hubbub.

my best friends Ben and Bonnie joined right away of course and they helped me make a bunch of ewok puppets . . . Bonnies are the ones with googly eyes and Bens is Logray. he spent so long on it he only got one done but i have to admit it is really cool . . . mine is Wicket OF COURSE.

Murky joined and made an ewok puppet to go with his Padmé (which has the coolest hat/crown things by the way) and he brought some of his buddies— Kristen, Pablo, and JW—and i finally talked Keril and Frankie from our M.A.G.I.C. Club into helping. that was nine and then this kid Brent wanted to join so i made an extra ewok for him.

so we had our own little mini-rebellion—ten ewoks—and all we had to do was take down a six-legged AT-AT.

i made up badges for everybody to wear that said: E.W.O.K.S.: EXCEPTIONALLY WONDERFUL ORIGAMI/KIRIGAMI SCULPTORS.

we decided to launch our trap between classes

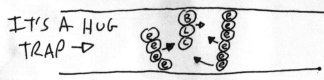

IT'S A HUG TRAP →

instead of before or after school. between classes is when it is most annoying to get stuck behind the BLC.

we figured out that after third period there would be six of us coming toward them and four of us coming up behind them. we were going to try to play that ewok trick where they smash the AT-AT between two logs. but we were going to be the logs if you know what i mean. what we had to do was make a six-person moving hug just like they did . . . and the ewoks on the other side would make another four-person hug and we would smoosh them in a hug-trap. as long as we did not budge the only way they could escape was by breaking their group hug.

but that was going to be the hard part because when the BLC glares at you or makes their little huffing noises youre going to want to budge big-time.

i gave the E.W.O.K.S. a pep talk with Mara Jade:

"i dont have to remind you if something goes wrong this is an EXCEPTIONALLY embarrassing way to die. but it can only go wrong if we let it.

103

our destiny is in our hands . . . and each of our destinies is in one anothers hands. if one of us crumbles we all will."

And Pad-mé added: "stand tall little ewoks and stand together!"

then we did it and . . . well we stood fairly tall.

there we were for one glorious moment: six of us stretching almost all the way across the hall and totally blocking the way but leaving just enough of a gap so that people could go through one at a time.

the BLC didnt even realize what was happening at first they are so used to everyone else moving out of their way. but. we. didnt.

and the other four came up behind. right on their butts!

finally the BLC HAD to either unhug or stop. they stopped.

and i was eye to eye with the worst of them: brenna!

"uh . . . move?" she said.

"yub nub!" said Wicket . . . right in her face!!!!!!!!!

they huffed and puffed and looked at us like we were idiots and we felt like idiots, especially when the kids who come up behind US starting huffing and puffing and looking too. thats when Ben cracked. he stepped away from the wall, letting a trickle of people through on the other side.

BEN

somebody behind me was going: "Remi, would you look out?" i was afraid to find out who it was. i had sort of forgotten that other people i knew were going to be mad at us for blocking the hall, not just the BLC.

"nar nar," i heard Murky saying. i felt Kym trying to let go of me. i held on to her.

"why are you acting like this?" asked Brenna.

"were just trying to show you what its like."

"what whats like?"

did they not know? could they really be ignorant of the havoc they caused in the hall?

i never found out.

"what on earth is going on here?" it was Rabbski.

after that it was all over in about a minute. i dont think Rabbski ever quite figured out that we were hug-walking to PROTEST hug-walking. i think she still thinks we were actually hug-walking.

but all that matters is that Rabbski banned hug-walking. it would be awesome to have that sort of power. to be annoyed by something and then just say "stop" and everybody has to stop. maybe i will be a principal someday it sounds like fun—well except when theres an origami rebellion.

anyway the BLC hates us now but frankly neither Wicket nor Mara Jade gives a piece of wampa poo what the BLC thinks and neither do i!

Harvey's Comment

I can't believe I'm saying this, but . . . MOST IMPRESSIVE! We had hug-walkers over in the seventh-grade hallway, too. They are the vilest creatures in the galaxy! And the Ewoks have beaten them! Will I . . . should I . . . okay, yes I WILL say it: Yub nub!

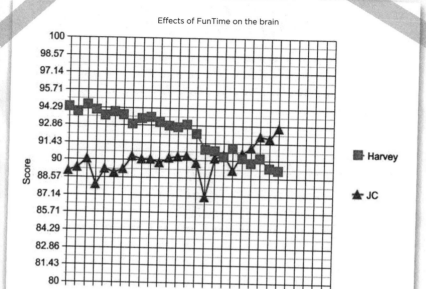

Effects of FunTime on the brain

Day 24

Harvey: 89.2%

JC: 92.7%

[Note: I wonder if Einstein could have survived FunTime?]

My Comment: Gee, maybe FunTime really is destroying Harvey's brain!

LANCE + AMY

R2 AND C-3PO KISS AND MAKE UP

BY LANCE

I think if there's one thing we can all agree on, it's that "Kiss This Kiss!" is the worst song in the history of music.

Actually, I guess that's not true. We can't ALL agree. Millions of people seem to think it's great because it is the number-one song and they play it on the radio ALL the time. I told you before how our gym teacher, Mr. Tolen, plays it during our warm-ups every morning.

I begged him to stop playing it, but he said it's catchy, has a good beat for doing jumping jacks, and he likes to play popular music that "the kids" like.

So I got the idea to get all of "the kids"—us—to tell him that they hate it, too.

NOWHERE WILL YOU FIND A MORE WRETCHED LACK OF TUNE +MELODY.

So at lunch, I was trying to convince everybody.

"It can be, like, part of our rebellion," I said. "If enough of us tell him that it stinks, I bet he'll switch."

But Amy said, "I think I'm actually starting to like it."

Amy? MY Amy? Likes "Kiss This Kiss!"? I couldn't believe it.

"NO WAY!" I said. "I don't think we can be friends anymore."

Now, of course you know I was just joking. Amy is my best friend and we hang out together all the time and we've even been on a few dates. (Nothing huge, just movies, etc. . . .)

Anyway, Amy didn't seem to realize I was joking, and she got really mad.

"Well, Lance, I'm sorry I'm just a stupid loser and I'm too dumb to appreciate beautiful music like that 'Jumpy Jack Flash' song."

Well, this was a cheap shot. I played that song for Amy on a date and I thought she had liked it. But now I realized that she had just been pretending to like it and now she was making fun of me for it . . . in front of everybody.

"It's 'JumpIN' Jack Flash'!"

"Oh, yeah, I know. My GRANDFATHER told me all about it. Apparently, that's the kind of junk they listened to when HE was a kid."

"JUNK?" I couldn't believe Amy had just called the greatest rock-and-roll song of all time "junk." For a second, I thought maybe we REALLY couldn't be friends anymore.

"How can you call 'Jumpin' Jack Flash' junk and say 'Kiss This Kiss!' is—"

But Harvey interrupted me.

"Hey, you guys really are like R2-D2 and C-3PO! Now, Amy, you just need to roll off into the desert in a huff. And then maybe some Jawas will come along and put a restraining bolt on Lance's mouth!"

"Harvey, why don't you—" I started, but then I realized Origami Yoda was talking.

"Learn to like that song Lance, too, will."

"What? No way!"

"Yes . . . the future I see . . . Lance, Amy driving in minivan . . . in the back kids are sitting . . ."

"WHAT???"

"'Kiss This Kiss!' on radio comes . . . Lance turns up volume . . . they laugh, sing along . . . roll eyes their kids do

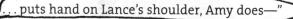

"...puts hand on Lance's shoulder, Amy does—"

"Enough!!!" shouts Harvey. "Stop before I puke!"

Then there was general commotion and discussion about whether Origami Yoda could really see the future that clearly, whether there would still be minivans and radios in the future, etc....

Then Amy whispered in my ear: "That sounds pretty good to me."

When I got home I downloaded "'Kiss This Kiss!'" and started memorizing the words.

Harvey's Comment

This has gone too far. Lance used to be pretty cool. ⟵
And actually Amy was kind of cool. But now that
they are in love, they are both completely annoying.

My Comment: Just for the record, I asked Dwight if
Origami Yoda could see me and Sara in the future and
he just gave me all that "Hard to see; always in motion
the future is" stuff.

UTINNI
THIS
UTINNI!

#1 SONG ON
THE JAWA
POP CHARTS...

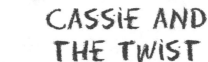

CASSIE AND THE TWIST

BY CASSIE

Everybody is all worked up about losing their electives, but they are mostly upset about things they wanted to do but hadn't actually started.

But those of us who were in chorus class and drama club got the most ripped off of anyone! Because we spent two months learning our play, *Olivia Twist*, and we never got to perform it.

(Also, I think Professor FunTime is even worse for those of us who actually know exactly how far off-key he is! Couldn't they have hired someone who could actually sing? He certainly can't act, so I don't know exactly what

they were looking for. And don't get me started on that screeching animated calculator!)

Olivia Twist was finally going to be my chance to star in a play. But I wasn't the only one who was excited. Amy, as the Artful Dodger, had all the funny lines, and she actually was pretty funny.

NORMAL HARVEY

EVIL HARVEY

And Harvey was actually really good for the first time, possibly because he was playing the totally evil character who makes me and the Artful Dodger and all the other orphans steal from Lance and Brianna, the old English gentleman and his really, really old wife.

And we had all practiced really hard and gotten good and knew our lines and were working on the dances . . .

And then last semester I found out that our drama teacher, Mrs. Hardaway, was leaving. Then we found out that there wasn't going to be a new chorus/drama teacher—just FunTime. And the play just suddenly ceased to exist.

But I didn't want it to.

So . . . then I heard that Dwight was back and he was leading some sort of rebellion. I didn't know if I really

wanted to join a rebellion, but I was willing to do it, if I had to, to star in a play.

And then once I heard more about FunTime and all that, I realized that there wouldn't be any more plays next year, either, unless we did something about it.

So I was ready to do something about it.

I went to see Dwight one day at lunch. His table was really crowded, so I waited until most of the people had left and Dwight was just sitting there, playing with his food.

"Dwight, I want to join your rebellion!"

"It's Captain Dwight," he said, which I thought was a little obnoxious.

But then Origami Yoda said, "Welcome you are. Waiting for you we have been. This paper you must take. Help you fold Sy Snootles Dwight will."

FUTURE SY SNOOTLES

"Uh, I have no idea what you're talking about . . ."

"Everyone in the Origami Rebel Alliance has their own origami character," explained Dwight. "Yoda's suggesting that you use Sy Snootles, the singer from Jabba's palace."

"Okay . . . but what else do I have to do?"

Dwight told me about how I was supposed to barely pass my Standards of Learning test.

"Uh, I hate to break it to you, but I barely passed last time anyway. Nobody's even going to notice."

"Judge you by the size of your score we do not," said Origami Yoda. "Dwight's score high was not, either."

"It's CAPTAIN Dwight," said Dwight.

"But what about the play? Is there anything we can do about that?" I asked.

"In front of you the answer is," said Origami Yoda.

"Uh, well, you and Dwight are in front of me."

"Well, right in front of you mean I did not."

"Look, Dwight, no offense, but I have never been able to figure out the Origami Yoda riddles. I can't believe I'm asking this, but maybe . . . Sherlock Dwight could explain?"

"It's CAPTAIN Sherlock Dwight," said Dwight in his crazy British accent. "And Yoda is quite correct. The answer is in front of you . . ."

"Uh, no, it's not!"

"Look in front of you, over my shoulder. Observe. What do you see?"

THE RETURN OF CAPTAIN SHERLOCK DWIGHT!

115

"Uh, the cafeteria?"

"Wrong! You see tables! You see bored kids! You see Lunchman Jeff cleaning up something nasty . . ."

Lunchman Jeff was at the far end of the cafeteria, near the stage, and he did appear to be cleaning up something nasty off the floor.

LUNCHMAN JEFF

"How did you know he was back there?"

"Elementary, my dear Cassie! Over your shoulder I noticed Lunchlady Ellen watching someone. She ignores all kids and most adults, but Lunchman Jeff always has her full attention . . . I noticed her wrinkle her nose in disgust and then giggle. They will share a laugh about this later . . . perhaps tonight at the Golden Corral buffet."

LUNCH-LADY ELLEN

"Okay, that is amazing, but it really has nothing to do with—"

"My dear, it has EVERYTHING to do with you and your play. I asked you what you saw and you said 'cafeteria.' But you are wrong even there."

"But it IS the cafeteria!" I said. I had forgotten how infuriating Dwight can be. Then it got worse.

He stood up. He began to shout. I began to try to hide under the table.

"This is not a cafeteria! THIS is a cafetorium!

"The tables? Your theater!

"The bored kids? Your audience!

"The stage? Your stage!"

Then he started to whisper: "Lunchman Jeff? The only person besides Rabbski and the night janitor with the keys to the side door that goes backstage!"

"You mean you want us to do the play here, during lunch?"

"Of course that's what I mean!"

"You think Rabbski will let us?"

"Ask her you will not. A rebel you are," said Origami Yoda. "BUT . . . practice more you must first. Tough crowd this will be."

So . . . I talked to the rest of the cast and it looks like we're going to do it. Brianna won't, of course, but Sara agreed to fill in for her. I asked Lunchman Jeff about the keys and he said he would "accidentally" leave that door unlocked on the day of the play.

So we've got a lot of practicing to do . . . which we're going to do every day before school in Miss Bauer's room. (She's cool about stuff like that.)

MISS BAUER... COOL...

So I'll let you know how it goes . . .

Harvey's Comment

I'm going to do it, but I think it's going to be a total disaster. our audience is going to be chawing on hamburgers and yakking at the top of their lungs.

My Comment: Well, I won't be yakking. Not if Sara's in it.

Kellen's Comment

TOMMY, YOU HAVE TOTALLY MISSED THE GENIUS PART OF THIS: ORIGAMI YODA HAS DONE IT AGAIN!!!
    HARVEY IS NOW GOING TO SPEND EVERY MORNING BEFORE SCHOOL IN MISS BAUER'S CLASSROOM, NOT IN THE LIBRARY WITH US!

NO HARVEY WOOT!

My Comment: OBD!* Sara will be in Bauer's room every morning, too. This is Origami Yoda's worst one ever!

    *Oh, Bantha dung!

NO SARA...??? WOOT!

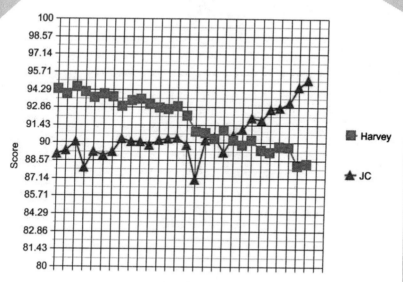

Effects of FunTime on the brain

Day 28

Harvey: 88.3%

JC: 95.1%

[Note: can ... feel ... brain ... dying ...]

CAROLINE

ORIGAMI YODA AND THE NEW, IMPROVED TIPPETT ACADEMY

BY CAROLINE

Tommy, I thought I was done writing stuff for your case file, now that Dwight has gone back to McQuarrie and I'm still here at Tippett...

But there have been some strange things going on here, which I figured you should know about!

I think some of the kids here were actually sorry to see Dwight go. Kimmy and Heather, those girls who were always trying to hug him, forgot about him the minute he walked out the door, of course. At first I was afraid they were going to look for another "special" kid to be friends with and hug, and if that kid was me, I was going to have to go into hiding.

KIMMY

HEATHER

CAROLINE

But they have a new project.

Before he left, Dwight had this weird good-bye thing. I didn't see it, but apparently the teacher, Miss Brindie, told the class Dwight was leaving and he told her he wanted to say good-bye to everybody. Of course, Kimmy and Heather came running up to try to hug him, but right when they got to him, he pulled two packages of stick-on googly eyes out of his coat pocket and handed them to the girls. Then he kept on pulling out packs. One for everybody in the class, even Miss Brindie.

Then Origami Yoda said, "Peel off they do, so vandalism it is not. Use them wisely . . . or unwisely . . . it matters not."

Then Dwight walked to the door and turned around, and Origami Yoda said, "May the Force be with you always . . ." Then he started to walk out and Miss Brindie said, "Dwight, there's still five minutes of class left." So he sat down on the floor right where he was and started fake snoring and didn't actually talk to anyone until the class really was over. After school his mom drove us both to Wendy's for farewell Frosties. (Although we're still planning to meet at Wendy's every week for a nondate anyway, so it wasn't really farewell.)

Okay, so anyway, I bet you can guess what Kimmy and Heather's new project is . . . Yep, sticking googly eyes on

HERE'S
LOOKING
AT YOU,
KID...

EVERYTHING in the school. And a bunch of the other people from Dwight's class are doing it, too, like those guys Tyler and Kendyll, who have found some pretty crazy places to put eyes. And the ones who aren't doing it gave their packs of googly eyes to the ones who are.

So now you never know where you're going to find a pair of googly eyes. Here are some of the places they've been found so far: light switches, toilet paper rolls, milk cartons, the rims of the basketball goals, Miss Brindie's rear end(!), a READ poster in the library of that actor from *Twilight* with the googly eyes over his eyes (a huge improvement), and the statue of Mr. Tippett's head in the entrance hall.

Of course, as soon as they started showing up, there was a Tippett Telegram (an announcement from the principal) reminding students that any sort of vandalism is against school policy. But apparently they are all ignoring this since Origami Yoda told them it wasn't really vandalism. But they are being super-careful not to get caught. So you never see them doing it; you just suddenly realize that your shoes are staring back at you!

It started looking like so much fun that some of us eighth-graders wanted to get in on it, too. But we didn't want to exactly copy the seventh-graders.

And then I remembered how Dwight had me wear those Band-Aids on my forehead for a while and I had some left in my locker. So . . . I kept some and handed the rest out to other eighth-graders! We went to work, and soon the school was covered in googly eyes and Band-Aids.

And then some sixth-graders started putting up fake mustaches they got from the gum ball machine at Food Lion.

And I have to tell you, it is SO MUCH FUN! It's actually a real challenge to think of good places and then figure out how to get them there without being caught.

I don't mean to brag, but if you ever come to Tippett, go in the auditorium and look at the ceiling, which is, like, fifty feet high—yep, there's a Band-Aid up there! Nobody has figured out how it could have been put up there (and I'm not telling), and the custodian hasn't figured out how to get it down!

So basically we've got a competition going with everybody to see who can do the wackiest stuff and Mr. Hutchinson, the principal, is going crazy, but I think a lot of the teachers are actually digging it. Tippett was just SO boring for everybody before and now it's actually fun! And believe it or not, I've actually started to make friends with some of these kids who I thought were snotty. (Which reminds me: Me, Kimmy,

MR. H.

REMIND YOU OF ANYBODY?

123

and Heather have a secret plan to plant fake boogers in Mr. Tippett's nose, as soon as we can get down to Sven's and buy some!)

So that's the crazy thing and the reason I sent this to be part of your case file. When Dwight was here, I was afraid Tippett was going to turn him normal. But now it's clear that Dwight actually turned Tippett ABNORMAL! And that is a huge, huge improvement!

Harvey's Comment

I don't get it. What's so funny about putting plastic eyes on stuff?

My Comment: Harvey, I KNEW you were going to say that!

I almost left this file out since it doesn't have anything to do with OUR rebellion, but then I decided to put it in because it's about how Dwight started another sort of rebellion over at Tippett. And I can hardly believe he got those Tippett kids to go nuts like that. Everybody always thinks they're a bunch of stuck-ups, but maybe they ARE kind of cool after all.

That's the crazy thing about this whole rebellion business. You can't always tell who's going to be a rebel and who's just going to be lame.

Some of the kids who complain about school all the time refuse to join the rebellion. And then along comes a cheerleadery type like Jen and SHE turns out to be a real rebel!

I COULDN'T THINK OF ANYTHING ELSE TO DRAW HERE... SO I DREW A PICTURE OF WILLY THE WALKING WAFFLE MEETING HIS NEW GIRL FRIEND, VANESSA THE ROLLER-SKATING MUSTACHE!

THE YEARBOOK REBELLION

BY JEN

Okay, I'm joining!

I know I said I wasn't going to join the first time you asked, but that was because I was only thinking about JV cheerleading, which wasn't affected since it's at the high school. And then I heard JV wrestling was getting canceled, and Tater Tot says JV football probably won't happen next fall, which means we won't have anyone to cheer for.

And now I am seeing how amazingly awful the FunTime changes are to *Concepts*.

My note: I had to ask Jen what "CONCEPTS" meant. CONCEPTS is the name of the McQuarrie M.S. yearbook. I guess I never noticed that before.

First, we don't have time to take any pictures since there is no actual yearbook class. Instead of getting photos for *Concepts*, we are stuck in FunTime just like everybody else.

Second, even when we do get a chance to use the cameras, there's nothing interesting going on!

Third, Mrs. Doughty is actually talking about dropping us down to the basic yearbook model. That's just everybody's school picture in black and white, plus four pages of color photos. Four pages!!! Last year we had thirty-two!

BUT if all we have are pictures of people sitting in FunTime class, then it's going to be hard to even fill up four pages!

So sign me up, and everybody else from *Concepts*, too.

Jen

oh, what a tragic loss to world literature if concepts doesn't come out!!! Just think of how empty our lives will be without pictures of all the obnoxious kids at this school! I'll cry myself to sleep if I don't have a full-color page of Tater Tot and his pals doing basketball drills . . .

My Comment: Okay, first of all, lay off Tater Tot. He's on our side! You're just jealous because he's smarter than you.

Also, notice that Jen said EVERYBODY from the yearbook. They have five kids from each grade on the yearbook staff, so that's a nice boost to our numbers.

AND one of those fifteen is Rhondella! Isn't it crazy that she ends up joining the rebellion anyway?

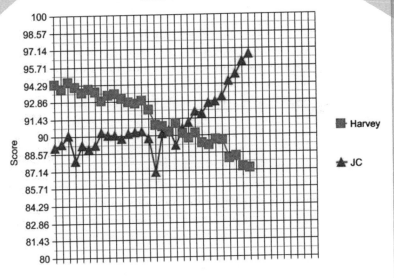

Effects of FunTime on the brain

Day 30

Harvey: 87.3%

JC: 96.7%

[Note: This is worse than I thought! Professor FunTime has taken over my brain. Every time I try to multiply a number I can hear him singing: "Multipli-k-tion is sweeping the nation!" I can't think anymore. I can't breathe! Help meeeee . . .]

KELLEN (ME!) LUKE

THiNGS GO NOSSSSSS SSSSSSSSSSSSSSS TRUL!!!!!!!!!!!!!!

BY KELLEN (AND TRANSCRIBED BY TOMMY)

The one thing around here that wasn't canceled was the spelling bee. I guess it would look bad if McQuarrie didn't send somebody to the county spelling bee.

I was pretty confident about the spelling bee this year. Last year, I won at McQuarrie and then went to the county spelling bee (where I got totally ripped off!).

So this year I was mostly thinking about how far I could go at the county level, not whether or not I would get there.

But I figured it couldn't hurt to ask Origami Yoda's advice. Sure, he may have sabotaged Marcie last year, but that was because she was a jerk about it. I knew he wouldn't do that to me . . . but then it seemed like he DID!

Here's what happened. I was studying my word list in the library before school on the day of the bee. Dwight came in, so I held up Luke Skyfolder and said, "Any words of advice, Master Yoda?"

"Whole wheat bread, healthier it is."

"Uh, no, I meant advice about the spelling bee today."

"Fight that battle do not!"

"What?"

"He said, don't fight that battle," explained Dwight.

"UH, yeah, I got that, but what's he talking about? Does he mean I shouldn't even compete in the spelling bee?"

"Hurt you it will . . . ," said Yoda.

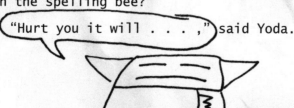

"What? I can handle a spelling bee. I mean, even if I lose, it's not that big of a deal. But I know I can win, and anyway, the top five go to county and I KNOW I can get in the top five."

"Hurt you it will . . ."

"Well, I'm still going to do it."

"What does Luke say?" Dwight asked.

So I thought about what Luke would say.

"I'm not afraid."

"You should be, you should be!" said Yoda in his growly, spooky voice.

"Oh, great," I said. "Just great. Thanks a lot for the support!"

I did think about dropping out. After all, Origami Yoda's advice has saved me before. But then I thought about trying to explain to my mom why I dropped out. Last year she was SO happy when I won. I knew she wouldn't be mad if I didn't win again, but she would go NUTS if I dropped out without even trying.

MY MOM

So I went ahead and did it.

They made an announcement before fifth period for the contestants to report to the band room—which they still call the band room even though there's no more band—and for everybody else to go to the cafeteria and sit down.

The band room was pretty crowded since there were twenty kids from each grade who were the top twenty in the grade-level spelling bees. Rhondella was one of the other seventh-graders in there, and I thought—well, you know, maybe we could talk. Maybe since we were both in the spelling bee, it would help somehow. But it was so crowded, I wasn't anywhere near her, but I could see her on the other side of the room talking to some eighth-graders.

RHONDELLA

Miss Bauer reminded us of all the rules, told us she was proud of us and all that, and then she said she would go see if they were ready for us to go up on the stage.

Well, the minute she left that meant there

ME

Rhondella

133

were no adults in the room and everybody started talking and I looked over at Rhondella to see if I could go talk to her . . .

And she was totally engaged in a PUBLIC DISPLAY OF AFFECTION with John Oxley, the huge, tall, nostrul eighth-grader!

I was like: BLU-RAY NOOOOOOOOOOOOOOO!

I don't want to go into details, but it was kissing and worse and it was the last thing I ever, ever, ever wanted to see, ever.

And then Miss Bauer came back and told us it was time to go onstage and we all went out and did the bee and I lost in the third round when I spelled "R-E-C-C-O-M-E-N-D."

I don't know if I lost because I was freaked out or if I would have misspelled that word anyway. And I don't really care, either.

When you get a word wrong they ring a bell and you have to leave the stage and go sit in a section of empty chairs and watch the rest of the spelling bee.

Guess who got rung out right after me?

Rhondella. ("Youthful," Y-O-U-T-H-F-U-L-L.) DUH! I could have gotten that one!

So we had to sit there next to each other for the whole rest of the thing. And then that nostrul John Oxley came in second and Rhondella was all WOOO-HOOO!

After it was all over and we were headed to our lockers, Dwight came over. I was about to be mad at him, but Origami Yoda just said, "The Force will be with you always."

Harvey's Comment

Kellen, don't worry, I'm not going to say anything nasty this time, because I have been in a similar situation myself and it really ... nostruls.

My Comment: Wait, what? Harvey in a similar situation??? With WHO?????

S-A-R-L-A-C-K-K

DING

ORIGAMI
REBEL
ALLIANCE
INSIGNIA
by
HARVEY
(NOTE. 2 pcs
of PAPER)

THE REBEL ALLIANCE

BY TOMMY

Being rebels was kind of fun, but we were missing our cool classes, we were still having to sit through FunTime every day, and teachers were starting to make plans for the Greenhill Plantation field trip!

We had all been going around trying to talk other kids into joining our Rebel Alliance and even though most kids said no, we had each started to collect a pretty long list of names.

Kellen was doing pretty well with his list,

partly because he had drawn this logo on it that said GIZMO-BUSTERS. It WAS cool and it seemed to work, but I tried to explain to him that this was about more than just defeating Gizmo—we were trying to get kids to take a stand against all the standardized test craziness so that we could get Rabbski to dump FunTime AND give us our classes and our field trip back.

He said that was too complicated and it was a lot easier to just ask kids if they wanted to smash Gizmo with a hammer.

Cassie had a huge list, because almost every kid who had been in the chorus or the band signed up right away. The band kids especially were complaining that if they couldn't take band in middle school, they wouldn't be as good as kids from the other middle school, Roddenberry M.S., once they all got to high school.

But it was obviously also because the band had been kind of a club for all of them and

DROOPY McCOOL

CLUB MEMBER SINCE: "A LONG TIME AGO..."

then they had been split up. So anyway, that was, like, twenty kids for each grade to add to our list.

And we got another nice boost when Jen, who had already brought in the yearbook staff, convinced the other JV cheerleaders to sign up. And those were all the most popular eighth-grade girls, so once they did it, a lot of other kids did, too.

As the lists got longer, it got easier and easier to sign new kids up. Being one of the first few kids to sign the list was scary, but once there's thirty kids on the list it's not that scary to become number thirty-one. I mean, even Rabbski couldn't put thirty-one kids in ISS. (For one thing, there's no room. Kellen says it's almost exactly like Leia's detention cell, but with a doorknob!)

Plus, as Origami Yoda kept reminding us, "Kick us out she cannot!" His theory was that Rabbski couldn't kick anybody out or even put us in ISS, because she needed us in class to learn the stuff that would be on the tests.

But to tell you the truth, I don't think the problem with most kids was fear of Rabbski. I think they just didn't believe we could change anything. School is whatever the adults say it is. If they say it's boring worksheets, then it's boring worksheets. So why bother? Why even waste the time signing your name?

UNCLE OWEN

And sometimes I understand how they feel. In fact, sometimes I feel exactly the same way.

But I had realized something. Fighting FunTime is better than FunTime. It isn't as bad to watch the Professor and Gizmo when you know you are actually working to bring about their downfall! And even if we never beat them, it's still better to know we tried.

And as far as the actual Standards tests . . . forget it. Whether we have enough people to really fight Rabbski or not, there is no way I'm going to actually bust my butt to try

to get a good score. As far as I'm concerned, that thing is the Dark Side and actually putting effort into it is like helping the Empire build their Death Star. And I'm not doing that.

I was starting to realize why Origami Yoda wanted me to have Foldy-Wan Kenobi: Sometimes this whole thing felt like a "darned fool idealistic crusade." And Obi-Wan is good at those.

Harvey's Comment

First, obi-Wan didn't say "darned." Second, obi-Wan LoSES!

My Comment: Great . . . thanks for the support, pal!

KELLEN'S COMMENT: WHAT IF WE ALL TOOK THE TEST USING #1 PENCILS? WOULD IT BLOW UP THEIR COMPUTER OR SOMETHING?

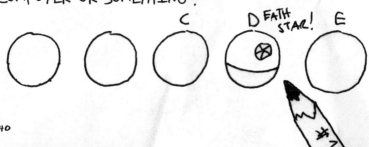

MRS. CALHOUN

THE SECRET MEETING OF THE REBEL ALLIANCE

BY MIKE, THE HOLOCRON KEEPER

Sara asked us rebel leaders to hold a secret strategy meeting in the library before school. Cassie actually canceled play practice so everybody could come.

Mrs. Calhoun, our cool librarian, let us use her office so we could be sure of privacy. It was jammed with about a million old book projects—like a dust-covered papier-mâché pig and a real mummified pickle with a hat—but we all crammed in there.

Rebels in attendance: Sara, Cassie, Tommy,

SOME PIG

Kellen, Harvey, Dwight, Amy, Lance, Remi, Murky, James Suervo, and . . . Jen.

[This is the first time Jen has been to one of our meetings. It was kind of weird sitting in that tiny room with somebody so . . . well, sort of like a school celebrity.]

When everybody was there, Dwight was busy poking the pickle with a pen . . . and then licking the pen. So Sara started:

Sara: I can't stand much more FunTime! And if we don't get our classes back soon, then it'll be too late to get them back at all! Our LEGO team is already light-years behind every other school! I think Fortune Wookiee speaks for everybody when he says, "WRUUUGH!"

Origami Yoda: Yes . . . truth there is in what you say. But rush in fools do—

Harvey: Not that again!

Origami Yoda: If we launch our rebellion before it has grown strong, crushed it will be!

Sara/Chewbacca: WRRRGGGHH!

Sara/Han Foldo: Right, Chewie!

Jen: OMG! I didn't know you guys actually used those finger puppets! They're so cute! I want one! Maybe Ventress? Can I be Ventress?

ORIGAMI VENTRESS

Harvey/Anakin: YOU know who Ventress is? Most impressive!

Sara: Uh, okay . . . like I was saying . . . that's why we need this meeting. To put all our lists together and see if we ARE strong enough yet.

Mike's note: Tommy told me I didn't need to write out this whole part. Basically, everybody handed Amy their lists of people they had signed up to be rebels and she split them up by grade and counted them. These are the results, with a few notes.

Seventh-Grade Total: 54
After every one of us had lectured, hassled,

and begged everyone we knew, we were still 6 short of the 60 we needed! And since there are 228 seventh-graders, you can tell that most of the people we asked had said no.

Eighth-Grade Total: 36

Not surprisingly, James Suervo—a.k.a. Hando Calrissian—only convinced a few eighth-graders to sign up. (But that's okay, James. WE think you're cool even if your fellow eighth-graders don't.) Jen actually brought in most of the ones we got.

Sixth-Grade Total: 48

Remi and Murky and the E.W.O.K.S. got a fair number of sixth-graders. And a lot of Tater Tot's pals are sixth-graders (who think they own the school after being here for six months).

Sara: Well, what do you think, Amy? Are the numbers close enough?

Amy: I can get a calculator and have a look,

but basically . . . no. We don't have sixty kids in any grade! We need to be able to tell Rabbski that we CAN and WILL defeat the Standards tests, not just MAYBE. We need more rebels!

Kellen: Geez, I feel like we've already asked everybody three times! Where are we going to get more?

Tommy: I guess we'll have to ask them four times . . .

James/Hando: I feel like I've let everyone down. I'm going to get you the other twenty-four eighth-graders . . . or die trying!

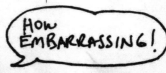

Amy: Can I give you some advice? Maybe don't use Hando to ask them. The ink has faded and now it just looks like your hand is dirty.

James: Great . . . Now I've let down Hando, too . . . He always likes to look his best. Maybe I better get a Sharpie and redraw it.

HOW EMBARRASSING!

Amy: I'm not sure . . .

Sara: Oh, just let him do it his way . . .
           Jen, you'll help him get some more
           eighth-graders, right?

Jen: Sure! Me and Origami Ventress will get
           right to work!

Sara: Well, you were right, Dw— uh, Captain
           Dwight. We do need to wait. But we also
           need to hurry up so we don't have to
           wait too long!

Origami Yoda: Worry not . . . The time for action
           approaches . . . possibly sooner than
           we wish.

Harvey's Comment

I'm pretty sure I said a bunch of really great stuff during this meeting! Why aren't you writing down the stuff I say?

My Comment: Dude, if Mike wrote down everything you said, this case file would be five hundred pages long! And you may have noticed that most of the stuff I said got cut out, too.

The important thing is that we all realized we needed to get busy.

The meeting broke up and we went out to try to find some more rebels . . . but one of us walked into a trap!

KELLEN'S COMMENT: ANYONE ELSE NOTICE THE BITE MISSING FROM THE MUMMIFIED PICKLE? I THINK DWIGHT TRIED TO EAT IT!

FRANK

STOMACH PUMP WE NEED STAT!

UH-OH!

BY SARA

Guys . . . something bad happened . . .

Today after school, I was standing in the bus line trying to recruit that girl Megan—you know, the one who calls herself Fred? Anyway, I was telling her all about it and then Ms. Rabbski walked by after shouting at some sixth-graders, and Megan/Fred said, "Hey, Ms. Rabbski, are you going to be mad if I sign this thing?" She didn't realize it was supposed to be secret!!!

"What 'thing' is that?" asked Ms. Rabbski, and she saw me trying to stuff my list inside my jacket. "Sara Bolt, is that 'thing' the 'thing' I think it is?"

Well, I couldn't lie to her! I don't like to lie to anybody, especially not the principal!

So I said, "Maybe." And she made me show it to her. She didn't keep it. She just glanced at it and handed it back. She didn't yell or anything. She just looked up at the sky for a minute and then said, "Thank you, Sara," and went back inside.

And Megan was like, "Oh, well, I guess she's not mad." And she signed the list.

But I knew that Rabbski WAS mad! Real mad!

Guys, I AM SO SORRY!!!

Harvey's Comment

Don't worry, Sara. That could have happened to any of us!

My Comment: Since when is Harvey being nice and understanding about stuff?

Anyway, he's right. That could have happened to any of us.

But now Rabbski knew what our plans were. Hopefully, she didn't realize that we didn't have enough rebels yet.

But just the fact that she knew about the rebellion was bad.

Origami Yoda had warned us that she would try to crush us . . . and she did!

principal RABBSKI

EMPRESS RABBSKI UNLEASHES THE ULTIMATE WEAPON

BY TOMMY

I forwarded Sara's e-mail to everybody, and most of the responses were the same as the one I got when I held up Foldy-Wan Kenobi:

"I've got a bad feeling about this!"

(Since almost every character from *Star Wars* says that line at some point, it's a pretty obvious thing for any of the puppets to say. Also, it was totally true! I DID have a bad feeling about this!)

We were all expecting to be called to the office first thing the next day to get yelled at, but we weren't. It turned out Rabbski had something much more clever in store. Something more diabolical. Something with PEPPERONI!

FUNTIME PIZZA PARTY!

Together we're going to ROCK those state Standards tests! So let's ROCK OUT with a FREE PIZZA PARTY!

Tuesday's FunTime classes will be held in the cafeteria, where we'll celebrate our TEAM SPIRIT with FREE PIZZA and ROCKIN' MUSIC from a special CELEBRITY GUEST!

Note: Sadly, not all McQuarrie students have chosen to be part of the team. These students are welcome to join us if they change their minds. Otherwise, they will report to Mr. Howell's classroom for an extra FunTime session.

"Wow, this is truly a tactic worthy of a Sith," said Harvey/Anakin. "A powerful reminder that she is not just Empress Rabbski, but also Darth Rabbskius!"

"Yeah, she's trying to find our weakest members and turn them against us," said Mike/ Mace Windu.

"I find it interesting that she's using FunTime as a punishment," said Captain Dwight. "That is an error we may be able to use against her later."

"Yeah, but what are we going to do right now?" asked Lance. "How are we going to stop everyone from going to get free pizza?"

"We'll all fold Admiral Ackbars and run through the school telling everyone 'It's a trap!'" said Kellen.

"Uh . . . we would, except that it would be TOTALLY EMBARRASSING," said Harvey.

"Actually, he's right," said Amy. "I think we'd lose more rebels than we'd gain that way."

"But what can we do?" I asked.

"Ah, there's the leadership we were waiting for," said Harvey. "Good to see, ol' Foldy-Wad is on top of things."

"Harvey, would you shut up? I wasn't even using Foldy-*WAN*; I was simply asking if anyone had a good idea. What can we do to fight this pizza party?"

"Nothing," croaked Origami Yoda.

"What???" I asked. "You mean we can't fight it?"

"No, nothing I mean!"

"Oh, good grief . . . here we go!" groaned Harvey.

"Wait a second," said Quavondo. "I think I know what Origami Yoda means. He's done this before. He says, 'Nothing,' but he means SOMETHING when he says it. Right now, he doesn't mean that we CAN'T do anything. He means that we SHOULDN'T do anything!"

"Yes . . . nothing you SHOULD do!" agreed Origami Yoda.

"But, everybody's going to defect if we don't do something," I said.

"Yeah, do you know how many people are going to show up for free pizza?" added Kellen.

"Let them," said Origami Yoda. "Back they will be . . . and in greater numbers."

"First of all," said Harvey, "that's Obi-Wan's quote, not Yoda's. Second of all, how can you be so sure that they won't defect?"

"Rockin'," said Origami Yoda.

"Huh?"

"I totally see what he's trying to tell us," said Quavondo. "It's the word 'Rockin'.' It's Rabbski's mistake. Her pizza party would have been a great idea if it had actually been fun, but the word 'Rockin'' is the tip-off that it's going to be lame."

"Wise this one is," said Origami Yoda. "What puppet has he chosen?"

"Kit Fisto!" said Quavondo.

"Good . . . good . . . the perfect Jedi for

155

"a spying mission he is. Go to the 'party' you must to be sure we are right . . ."

Harvey's Comment

[Quickly folds Grand Moff Tarkin puppet.] We're taking an awful risk . . . This had better work.

My Comment: That's an understatement! So far, just about every "rebel" we've signed up is planning on going to the pizza party tomorrow. I can't believe they are willing to give up everything for a slice of pizza!

Those of us who are left really feel like the Jedi Council in REVENGE OF THE SITH now . . . with the Empress turning everyone against us. And on top of that, we all have to go have a SPECIAL FunTime with Mr. Howell while everyone else gets pizza!!!

EVEN WORSE... THESE JACKED-UP JEDI CHAIRS HURT THE BE-HIND!

KIT FISTO AND THE ROCKIN' GOOD TIME!

BY QUAVONDO

Okay, I'm taking notes during the pizza party.

Keeping Kit Fisto in my shirt pocket. Don't want to draw attention and have Rabbski send me back to Mr. Howell's class with the rest of you.

So far, it looks like almost everybody is here. The cafeteria is packed!

There's been a lot of discussion about whether the pizza will be Domino's or Papa John's. A few people have been hoping for Shaffer Brothers New York Style, which is the best pizza place in town, but I think they probably wouldn't be able to make enough for all of us.

POCKET
FULL
OF
FISTO! →

They've opened the doors to the food lines! People are pushing to get to the front of the line . . .

PIZZA↓

Now they're coming out the other side with . . . pizza boats!

PIZZA BOAT↓

I repeat, PIZZA BOATS! This is not restaurant pizza. It is cafeteria pizza, and it is not even real pizza—it is pizza boats, the evil twin of a good slice of pizza.

The news about the pizza boats is spreading through the crowd. A lot of people have gotten out of the lines. It's just not worth standing in line for a pizza boat!

PEPPERONI↗

When will they learn that toasted yet soggy bread with tomato sauce and cheese on it is not REALLY pizza?

Turk-y-Roni↓

Oh, my mynocks! It's worse than I thought! The pepperoni isn't actually pepperoni! It's HealthYums Turk-y-roni!!!!

Tommy's note: Quavondo has about five pages of notes about the pizza boats . . . I think we can safely skip ahead to the "entertainment."

Principal Rabbski has walked out onstage . . .

People are still grumbling about the pizza boats, so Rabbski has to do her clapping thing to get everybody's attention. It doesn't really work, so she does it again—this time banging her hand against the microphone—and it makes this loud shriek.

"We're throwing this party to let you know how proud we are of all of you for working so hard for the last month," she says into the mic. "I know that watching the FunTime videos isn't always the most exciting thing in the world, so we've rustled up some live entertainment for you! Please give a big McQuarrie welcome to . . ."

Hey, Tommy, can you guess? I bet you can guess, can't you?

"... Mr. Good Clean Fun and his pal, Soapy the monkey!"

Music starts blaring out of the speakers. And I mean blaring! It's some kind of country song, I guess.

Wait. The music just stopped.

And now it has started again, but now it's, like, a hip-hop beat or something . . .

Mr. Good Clean Fun and Soapy just ran out onstage. (Well, only Mr. GCF actually ran, of course.)

And now they are rapping. I'm glad I brought Kellen's recorder thingy for this so I can get all the words:

Mr. GCF:	FunTime! It's one time
	That you'll think is the best!
	'Cause it's all about
	Fun ways to beat the test!

MOON-
WALK

Soapy:	Give us a minute.
	We'll teach you to win it.
	We're gonna make McQuarrie number one!
	You won't have no trouble
	Fillin' out those bubbles
	'Cause you learned in a way that was fun!

Now Mr. GCF is yelling, "Break it down!"

He keeps clapping Soapy's paws (?) over his head like we're supposed to start clapping, too.

Now he's trying to teach us to chant "Do your best, on the test."

"When I say 'do your' you say 'best!' Do your . . .

"When I say 'on the' you say 'test!' Do your . . . on the . . ."

Nobody is doing it.

Wait—some eighth-graders have started yelling, but

. . . .. cricket chirp .... cricket chirp ..... cricket chirp

160

they're yelling "TEST!" when they're supposed to say "best." And vice versa.

Mr. GCF doesn't even seem to care. Maybe he's just glad that he's not being interrupted by either Cheetos or a snot trooper this time, but frankly it doesn't seem like his heart is really in this. And Soapy the monkey definitely doesn't seem to care whether we do our best or not.

NICK, THE INTER-RUPTING CHEETO!

Ah . . . It's finally over!

Oh, no . . . no . . . please no . . . Dwight, send your squirrels to save us! He's starting another song! This one's about getting a good night's sleep before the test! And what to eat for breakfast . . .

I think I'll stop taking notes. Yoda was definitely right: "Rockin'" is the opposite of "rocking." I'm just sorry Kit Fisto had to hear this . . .

THE KID'S RIGHT . . . I HONESTLY COULDN'T GIVE A *#!@-幼#&!

The horror! The horror!

My Comment: It's hard to believe that those of us who watched FunTime with Mr. Howell were actually the LUCKY ones!

¡VIVA LA REVOLUCIÓN!

BY TOMMY

After the pizza party was over, everybody was griping and complaining and saying they only went for the pizza and they were still with us. And a bunch of people who hadn't been with us before were ready to sign up.

Plus, now that we were no longer operating secretly, it was a lot easier to ask around, and Remi and Kellen even put up some signs.

It worked! Two days after the pizza party, we had the numbers we needed!

Fifteen new sixth-graders joined, to give us sixty-three!

We got the six seventh-graders we needed, plus eighteen more. That gave us a total of seventy-eight!

Fourteen new eighth-graders joined, so that gave us fifty. Still not enough, but close, and still enough to be a serious threat to the average.

So, Origami Yoda was right. We were now more powerful than ever. We had numbers that Rabbski could not ignore. And Captain Dwight insisted that now was the time to let her know it.

So . . . we did.

Ms. Rabbski,

We are back. This time there are many, many more of us. We are the Origami Rebel Alliance and there are 191 of us!

Our feelings about FunTime and the loss of our electives, sports, and field trips are still the same.

What has changed is our plan.

We will not flunk the tests. We will pass the tests, but just barely. Each of us will take a tiny bit off the average. It will have the same effect. (See the attached sheet for the math behind this.)

The last time we tried this, you thought we were being traitors to our school. No! We are trying to make it good again.

We don't want to sabotage the school, but we are more than willing to sabotage the tests.

You and the school board may care about those test scores, but we don't. We do care about art and band and sports and all the other things we have lost. So if anything, it is us, the Origami Rebel Alliance, who are faithful to what McQuarrie Middle School is supposed to be!

Also, we just can't stand another day of the singing calculator and the break-dancing dictionary!

Signed,
The Origami Rebel Alliance:
63 sixth-graders
78 seventh-graders
50 eighth-graders

THE SECOND MEETING WITH RABBSKI

BY MIKE, THE HOLOCRON KEEPER

So, there we were . . . back in Rabbski's office. This time, when they called our names over the PA, everybody knew why. I kind of wish the other kids had cheered instead of just staring at me as I walked out.

Rabbski didn't call everybody. Just me, Tommy, Kellen, Harvey, Dwight, Amy, Lance, and Sara.

Rabbski: Oh, goody! I see we still have the puppets. Wonderful. And I see that you have all the good guys . . . So I guess that makes me . . . who? Emperor Palpatine?

YEP!

Harvey: You know who Emperor Palpatine is?

Rabbski: Listen, Harvey, I was watching *Star Wars* before you guys were born. I know all about the Emperor . . . and, listen, I'm not the Emperor. I'm just your principal and I'm just trying to help you kids get an education, despite all of your puppets and petitions and other craziness.

[She held up our letter.]

Rabbski: I am really disappointed by this. You've talked almost two hundred kids into NOT doing their best. That goes 100 percent against the McQuarrie Pledge, which we all live by here and which you all agreed to follow: "We treat each other with respect. We . . .

[She recited the ENTIRE McQuarrie Pledge from memory. It goes on forever. I'm not going to type it all out here! So I'm skipping to the end . . .]

Rabbski: "AND we will work as a team to make

McQUARRIE VIKING
TAKING McQUARRIE
PLEDGE...
←

McQuarrie the best school in Lucas County!"

Origami Yoda: Doing that we are. Teaming up we are to get rid of the FunTime Menace and restore balance to the school.

Rabbski: Balance to the school? Do you realize what happens if we don't get our accreditation back? If we fail those tests again, there may be more budget cuts, parents may transfer their kids to other schools, where the scores are higher . . . which would mean still more budget cuts. There may be personnel changes. Do you realize what that means? Teachers could get transferred. I could get transferred . . .

[Long pause. I guess one of us should have said we didn't want her to get transferred away, but nobody did.]

Rabbski: But that's not what this is about. This is about each of you making the right choice for yourself and for your school. And the right choice is doing your best. Isn't that what Yoda would say? I can't imagine Yoda telling Luke, 'Try not. Your best you must not do . . .' This is serious business. It's not a game. McQuarrie needs to pass those tests. If we can get the scores up and keep them up for a few years, then the electives can come back—

Harvey: A few years? We'll be gone by then!

Rabbski: I'm asking you to think not about yourselves, but about the school. I'm proud of this school. And I'm asking you to take pride in it, too. I'm asking you to stop distracting the other students with your petitions and puppets.

But also, yes, it IS for you. These are things you need to know. AND your poor test scores will be part of your permanent record. Remember when Yoda told Luke not to go fight Vader,

UH... I DON'T REMEMBER SAYING "KNUCKLE-DOWN.

but to knuckle down and finish his studies? That's what I'm telling you today.

C'mon! Get the most out of FunTime and then ace those tests for me, for your school, and for yourselves. This is for your futures. Okay?

[She shouldn't have said FunTime again. The thought of going back to FunTime was too awful to bear!]

Mike (me): [Kinda too loud.] YOU KNOW WHAT, MS. RABBSKI? I THINK—

[Just then Mace Windu gave me a look. You know those looks he can give. It was a look that said: Keep it cool. So I did.]

Mike (me): [Calmly.] I don't think these tests are going to do me any good in the future.

Kellen: Yeah, like, in the future, I want to go to comic book school. Won't it look better on my permanent record if I take art class now instead of sitting

there watching Professor FunTime and
his singing calculator?

Rabbski: Another smart aleck!

Kellen: No! I'm not being a smart aleck! I'm
serious!

Rabbski: NO! I'm the one who is serious. You
kids haven't realized how serious this
is. You're too young to understand it
all. That's why adults have made these
decisions for you. School boards, the
state Department of Education, the U.S.
Department of Education, Congress,
even the president, who signed the
whole thing . . . These aren't just
my crazy ideas. They are the LAW! This
is bigger than me and it's bigger than
you. You simply don't have a choice.

[I didn't really know what to say. I was starting
to feel pretty dumb for trying to fight something
that big.]

Now, I'll toss out this letter, too,
and you'll go back to class, nobody

ALL IN FAVOR OF THE SINGING
CALCULATOR LAW SAY "AYE . . . "
. . . CRICKET . . . CHIRP . . .

OH,
POOP
AGAIN!

will be in any trouble, and we'll drop
the whole thing. Okay?

[Nobody said anything.]

Rabbski: Okay?

Origami Yoda: Okay it is not!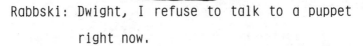

Rabbski: Dwight, I refuse to talk to a puppet
right now.

Captain Dwight: Well, I refuse to talk to anyone
who does not address me as Captain
Dwight.

Rabbski: RRRGGGH! This has got to stop! Can't
you kids be serious?

Harvey: [Muttering.] You're the one who is
doing a Wookiee impression . . .

[Ms. Rabbski made a face like . . . like I don't
know what. I would not have been surprised if
Force lightning had shot out of her fingers and
fried Harvey. Finally, she sat down and took some
deep breaths. She counted to ten out loud.]

Rabbski: Okay . . . Harvey, you may go directly
to the ISS room.

Harvey: Bu—

Rabbski: NO! Don't say a word. You go to ISS. The rest of you will go back to class. There's no use talking to you about this anymore. I tried to be nice. I tried to talk. I even tried giving you free pizza. But I give up. Now, if you'll excuse me, I have some phone calls to make . . . to your parents.

Captain Dwight: PARENTS???

Rabbski: Yes. Since I'm getting nowhere with you, it's time to let your parents know about—

Captain Dwight: [Jumping around.] NO! NO! I'm sorry! I'm sorry! Don't call! I give up!

Origami Yoda: No, Captain Dwight! Don't give up!

Dwight: [Bawling and throwing his cape on the floor.] I'm not Captain Dwight! The rebellion is over! [Runs for the door.] Don't call! Don't call!

Origami Yoda: Dwight! Go back!

Dwight: [Now in the outer office.] No!

PAUSE + REFLECT
ON THIS SAD SIGHT
BEFORE TURNING PAGE...

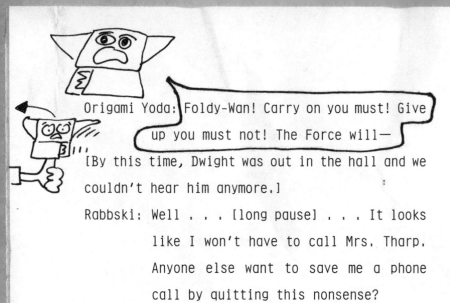

Origami Yoda: Foldy-Wan! Carry on you must! Give up you must not! The Force will—

[By this time, Dwight was out in the hall and we couldn't hear him anymore.]

Rabbski: Well . . . [long pause] . . . It looks like I won't have to call Mrs. Tharp. Anyone else want to save me a phone call by quitting this nonsense?

[Everybody looked around for a minute.]

Tommy/Foldy-Wan: We have made a commitment to the origami rebellion . . . a commitment that is not easily broken.

Sara/Fortune Wookiee: YRRYAHH!

Amy/R2-D2: Beep!

Lance/C-3PO: Oh, R2! Are you sure?

Amy/R2-D2: [Whistles.]

Lance/C-3PO: Oh, all right . . .

Mike (me): [Very calmly.] Uh, yeah, I agree with Tommy, too.

Luke Skyfolder: I'm sticking with you, Foldy-Wan. There's nothing for me here now. I want to learn the ways of the Force and become a Jedi like—

Rabbski: All right! Enough! Like I said, I'm done talking to you. I'm ready to discuss disciplinary methods directly with your parents. Now, if you'll excuse me, it looks like I have a lot of telephone calls to make.

Harvey's Comment

Well . . . Foldy-Wan finally said something. And I have to admit it was pretty good. It would have been nice if he could have saved me from ISS, but Rabbski was so mad at me I guess I was unsavable.

Normally, the worst part of ISS is sitting in there with nothing to do, thinking about having to take the note home for your parents to sign. But this time, I knew I was going to have to explain the note AND Rabbski's phone call AND the whole plan to do bad on the tests.

Plus, guess who the ISS supervisor was? That's right, Mr. Howell. Just me and Mr. Howell in a tiny room for an hour! I tried to explain the whole thing to him, and surprisingly, he did listen, but you can guess how sympathetic he was. All he did was grunt!

My Comment: That sounds pretty bad, dude! But all of us were pretty miserable all day, knowing that when we got home we were going to have to face our parents . . .

Everybody except Mike, that is. He was pretty cool about the whole thing . . .

MACE, MIKE + HAPPINESS

ME AND MACE WINDU

BY MIKE, THE HOLOCRON KEEPER

USUAL MIKE

I bet everyone has been wondering something: Why isn't Mike crying?

I mean, these meetings with Rabbski are very stressful and things are going terribly and our parents are about to get involved. Usually, I'd end up crying, right?

Well, as I have tried to explain a million times: They aren't boo-hoo tears; they are mad tears. There's a difference. Just like some people cry when they are happy, I cry when I get mad. Well, sometimes I sort of freak out, too.

TEAR TYPES

 BOO-HOO

MAD

 HAPPY

 CONFUSED

 ACCIDENTALLY RUBBED HOT SAUCE IN EYE

And that usually gets me in trouble, and that makes me madder and makes me cry more and freak out more, and so on . . .

Well, not this time. Not with Mace Windu here to help!

See, when something happens, like Rabbski yelling at us, and I want to start yelling back . . . Mace Windu always stops me.

He's like: Play it cool, dude. Just Play. It. Cool.

And I'm like: But I AM right this time! I NEED to say this.

And he's like: No, you don't. But you DO need to do your job. Listen instead of talk. Think instead of bawl. Make the Holocron. And be cool . . . Just BE cool.

And as you know, Mace Windu is the coolest guy in the galaxy. And some of his coolness has been rubbing off on me.

Instead of a freak-out . . . I just keep it cool.

Instead of jumping out of my seat and yelling,

"This is so nostrul!" I just sit there and play it cool and make some notes. I have survived the meetings and the announcements and even the awful TV show, and now I can calmly look back and realize that freaking out wouldn't have changed Rabbski's mind or stopped FunTime anyway. But maybe by playing my role in the rebellion, I actually AM doing something to change things!

Origami Yoda was great and he did help keep me from crying a few times, but Mace Windu has helped me get past all of that, hopefully forever! I am taking him everywhere with me now and I haven't freaked out about FunTime or anything else in ages!

GOOD
BETTER!

And I know that when Rabbski calls my mom and my mom asks me to explain it, I will be able to stay cool and calm and tell her the whole thing. Frankly, I even think I can convince her to take my side.

Origami Yoda was right. I needed to be the Holocron Keeper and I needed Mace Windu. Because Mace is cool and now so am I!

KEEP
COOL
AND
CARRY
A
PURPLE
LIGHTSABER!

cool? Dude, I wasn't going to say anything, but you
have been behaving like a rabid wampa lately.

You're, like, just about to say something. And then
you hold up Mace Windu, which, by the way, happens
to look like a rabid wampa, and you start muttering
to yourself and then you just sit there and don't say
anything. Real cool!

WHAT
DID
I DO?

OFFENDED
WAMPA

My Comment: Mike, let me borrow Mace Windu . . .
so I don't lose my cool yelling at Harvey!

As usual, he misses the whole point!!!!

Origami Yoda/Captain Dwight made a genius decision
when he gave Mike Mace Windu. Mike needed Mace;
otherwise he would have ruined this whole rebellion for
all of us a long time ago by screaming at Rabbski and
then bawling.

It's just kind of sad when you find out what did
happen to Mike and Mace when they faced his mom.
In fact, the whole next chapter is going to be pretty
sad . . .

SNIFF... THESE
ARE BOO-HOO
TEARS!

WRATH OF THE PARENTS!

BY EVERYBODY

Tommy: Obviously, the best strategy here was to tell our parents BEFORE they got the phone call from Rabbski. This would give us a chance to tell our side of the story, before Rabbski starting in about us "disrupting the learning environment." (That's her all-time favorite phrase.)

But it's not exactly easy to talk to my parents. They don't sit still very often. The best I could do was to try talking to my dad on our way to pick up my brother from swim practice.

TOMMY'S DAD

TOMMY'S BROTHER
→
WHO DID/DOES
COMPLAIN ABOUT
EVERYTHING!

His reaction: "I don't understand. Your brother never had any problem with those tests. I never heard him complaining, much less starting a riot."

"It's not a riot. It's a rebellion."

"Well, I don't have time to deal with it right now," he said as we pulled into the parking lot. "I've got to talk to Coach Ryan. Why don't you just wait in the car?"

At least he wasn't mad. And then when we got home there was a message from Rabbski on the answering machine. Basically, she said that I was one of several students "disrupting the learning environment" and my parents needed to come to a meeting at school about it on Thursday night.

"Thursday night? That's just great. Your brother has a swim meet Thursday night!"

Lance: I tried a different strategy. I decided not to say anything about it at all. And guess what? Rabbski never called! I'm not in trouble! That's what I call waffles!

WAFFLES, MAN!

Harvey: I decided to go with facts and figures. I showed them the data from my science fair project.

From the beginning, where I was scoring 94.3 percent on BrainBusters2Lite, to the latest score, which was:

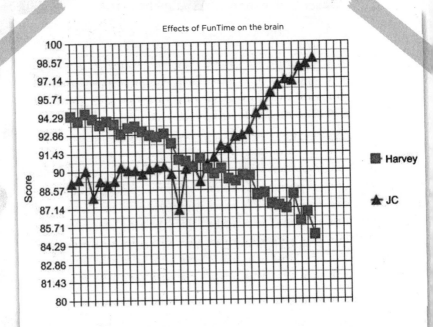

Effects of FunTime on the brain

Day 35: Harvey: 85%, JC: 98.7%

It didn't go over so well.

My dad called it "bad science." (You know he's a biology professor at Roanoke College, right?)

He said he thought maybe I was trying to do bad on BrainBusters2Lite because I wanted to prove my point. I told him I wasn't. But he said that even if I didn't do it on purpose, I probably wasn't really trying as hard as I used to. He said all scientists have to deal with stuff like this. That's why they usually don't experiment on themselves.

Plus, he said that experimenting on just two people isn't enough to prove anything anyway. He said it was a "small sample size," which made it "more likely to be biased."

So, not only did it not convince him ... he also says I need to start a brand-new science fair project using better methods!

(Kellen, can you draw Anakin getting his Darth Paper helmet put on for the first time?)

NOOOOOOOOOOOOOOOOOOOOOOOOOO
OOOOOOOOOOOOOOOOOOOOOOOOOOOOOOOOOOOOOOOO
OOOOOOOOOOOOOOOOOOOOOOOOOOOOOOOOOOOOOOOO
OOOOOOOOOOOOOOOOOOOOOOOOO!!!!!!!!!!!!!!!!

My note: Can I just point out that Harvey's cousin's latest score is higher than Harvey's all-time high score? So that makes Harvey the dumb cousin!

185

Kellen: My mom is furious! She took away my PlayStation and said I can't use her computer to play Minecraft anymore until I "find a way to fix this whole mess."

I told her we were trying to fix it. She said she didn't like my attitude.

Sara: Well, it's a good thing my grandmother was at our house for supper last night. My mom started chewing me out, but then my grandmother was like, "Don't you remember when you were part of that high school walk-out?"

SARA'S GRANDMA

"That was different!" said my mom.

SARA'S MOM

"Oh, sure," said Grandma. "That was about something REAL important: Bart Simpson T-shirts."

GIVE ME BART OR GIVE ME DEATH!

"Mom," said my mom to her mom, "it was about free speech!"

Turns out that my mother and a bunch of kids in her high school all walked out of school and stood around in the parking lot to protest the school dress code, which for some reason banned Bart Simpson T-shirts. (I have no idea why.)

After they argued about it for a while, my mother

turned to me and said, "Don't think you're off the hook, young lady! I want to hear what your principal has to say first."

But at least she stopped yelling at me . . . until Thursday night.

Quavondo: It's not fair that Rabbski called my parents, because I wasn't even there when she gave you guys a chance to give up! I didn't even know she was going to call. Just all of a sudden the phone rang and my mom answered and then started glaring at me!

CRAZY SISTER

Oh, man . . . I knew I shouldn't have joined the rebellion. My parents are "disappointed," and my crazy sister is furious at me for talking her into signing up, because she got in trouble, too!

AMY'S MOM

Amy: My mom was like, "Did Lance get you mixed up in this? I knew that boy was going to be a problem! You're just too young to be going out on dates." So I was like, "Can I still go to the movies with him on Saturday?" And she said, "We'll see what happens at this meeting . . ."

Lance's note: That's NOT waffles!

Mike: Guys, I can't be the Holocron Keeper anymore. And I can't be part of the Origami Jedi Rebellion. I'm going to be lucky if I can even keep going to school at McQuarrie. My mom is talking about sending me to church school!

I told my mom about everything on our way home from my RightWayKidz meeting. Well, she didn't even seem to care that much about the rebellion or the tests. She was only interested in one thing: Origami Yoda.

And not in a good way.

MIKE'S mom

She asked me about a million questions about him. I didn't see any reason not to tell the truth, so I told her all about how Dwight used Origami Yoda to help me play baseball better and to predict the future and all that stuff.

"And how do you think a finger puppet could do all of that?" she said.

"The Force?" I said.

She stopped the car. She actually pulled over into the CVS parking lot.

"I've had some concerns about those *Star Wars* movies in the past, Mike, especially that cartoon thing you watch. Now I see that that was a huge mistake. Well, that is all over. You can go back to watching VEGGIETALES."

"VEGGIETALES? What? Why?"

Well, it turns out that she thinks Origami Yoda is some sort of black magic or something. She said following a finger puppet was like worshipping an idol—which is against one of the Ten Commandments—and getting mixed up with predictions and fortune-telling is the first step on the road to witchcraft and the occult, which is, like, devil worship or something.

HO∪
SHALT
NOT
-OLD
ODAS!

WITCH-
CRAFT?

She wasn't even that mad about it, at least not at me.

"I don't blame you, Mike. This is what happens when they don't let you pray in school. Something else is bound to creep in. I just wish there was a good church school near here, like the Lighthouse School your cousins go to."

(My cousins all go to this church over near

Crickenburg. On Sunday they go to morning services and then on weekdays they go right back to their church to have school. They love it, but then again they love everything.)

Anyway, she finally drove the rest of the way home. She made me turn over my Origami Mace Windu and promise not to listen to anything Origami Yoda had to say. And at the end of the school year she's going to decide whether I can come back next year or go somewhere else . . . maybe even all the way to the Lighthouse!

And she confiscated all my *Star Wars* stuff until I'm "old enough to understand that there is no Force."

Well, without Mace I didn't exactly keep cool. I may have yelled and had some mad tears, and then I accidentally said a bad word. Then she WAS mad!

So . . . bye, everybody. Sorry I can't be the Holocron Keeper anymore and I'm out of the rebellion! Sorry! I wish I could be there at the meeting with you! I'll be at home . . . but the Force is with you . . .

Harvey's Comment

I don't get it. Does his mom think origami Yoda is, like, the devil or something? A satanic paperwad?

My Comment: I don't know exactly. I tried to talk to him about it, but he said he isn't even supposed to talk to us anymore.

As I see it, there's only one way out of a mess like this: Ask Origami Yoda what to do.

But that's the one thing we can't do, because Dwight isn't bringing him to school anymore and isn't talking to anybody except to say, "Purple."

Man, it is a DARK time for the rebellion!

YAY! THAT MEANS IT'S A DARK CHOCOLATE TIME FOR ME, JEDI SCUM!

Yummy!

CHOC

TWIX

EMPRESS RABBSKI

• RABBSKI MEETS
* WITH OUR PARENTS!

BY TOMMY (TEMPORARY HOLOCRON KEEPER
UNTIL WE GET MIKE BACK)

When we all got there Thursday night, Ms. Rabbski greeted everybody and acted real friendly to the parents. But also grim . . . sort of grim-friendly, like people were at my uncle's funeral.

We were all nervous and not really talking much. But then Kellen started yanking on my jacket.

"Look!" he whispered.

It was Mr. Howell!

"What is he doing here?" I whispered back.

GENERAL HOWELLOUS!

"I guess he's Rabbski's backup! If we try to say anything, she'll sic him on us like when the Emperor sends out General Grievous to do his dirty work!"

We all went into Mr. Howell's classroom and we all sat in desks, even our parents. We had agreed not to bring any origami because none of us thought it would impress our parents. But without the origami, the Origami Rebel Alliance didn't seem very powerful. We were just a bunch of kids about to get stomped on by adults.

Rabbski stood up at the front. She was wearing one of those power suits of hers. It was clear that SHE was in charge and the rest of us . . . even our parents . . . were there to listen.

So she started in again about taking down the dumb banner and how her dream is to see McQuarrie be the best school in the county and how it nearly broke her heart when our scores came in so low last year. (She has a heart?)

POWER SUIT

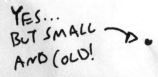

YES...
BUT SMALL
AND COLD!

We were about to barf from all the baloney she was saying . . . but our parents weren't. They were nodding their heads! Rabbski was totally making her point, and she was making it sound like anyone who wasn't helping her must be a bad, bad person. A traitor! It was just like when the Emperor turned the Senate against the Jedi!

 And then—just when it seemed like we were about to get vaporized by the Death Star—something happened . . . the Force was with us!

"Your children's education is SO important to us . . . That's why we have started FunTime," Rabbski was saying. "FunTime is an award-winning educational program developed by—"

Right then the TV came on and the FunTime song came blaring out super-loud!

"FunTime! Every minute, every second will . . . help you FOCUS on the FUNdamentals!"

"What's going on?" yelled Rabbski.

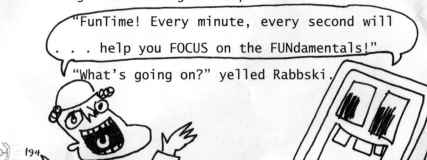

The song kept playing. The singing calculator kept singing. And Professor FunTime was doing some disco moves!

GREAT LYRICS, HUH?

Then suddenly it was off.

"Whew, ha-ha," Ms. Rabbski said. "Sorry about that . . . But as I was saying—"

The TV came back on.

"FunTime! We'll getcha ready for your test! We'll help you do your very best!" sang the calculator.

Professor FunTime was doing the robot dance!

"I'm Professor FunTime!" he shouted.

"And I'm Gizmo!" shrieked the calculator.

Rabbski stomped over to the TV and pushed the power button. It went off. She took a couple of steps, and it came back on!

"Who's doing this?" demanded Rabbski, pushing the off button again. "Does someone have the remote?"

We looked around, but nobody was holding the remote.

DOING "THE ROBOT"

HOW RUDE!

"Well, it's not here. Someone must have it. I can't believe one of you would act this way while your parents are here. Tommy, this has your name written all over it."

"It's not me!" I said.

The TV popped on and then back off. Just long enough to prove that I wasn't doing it.

"Kellen, give me the remote," said Rabbski.

"Me?" said Kellen. "I don't have anything." And he stood up and pulled out his pockets and patted himself all over.

"Harvey?"

"I would never willingly listen to that music," said Harvey.

And just as he said it, the show came on AGAIN!

"My name is Gizmo and I'm here to say, I'll teach you to divide the easy way!"

This time it just kept playing until Rabbski went over and unplugged the TV from the wall.

"Okay, maybe we can get on with it now," said Rabbski.

But she was no longer in charge.

"Ms. Rabbski," said Kellen's mom. (And you should hear the way she said it!) "Is that egregious show on that TV the 'educational' program you told us about?"

"Yes, that's the, er, digital media portion of FunTime. There are other components, including challenging knowledge-building exercises."

"Worksheets," Sara whispered to her mother, loud enough for everyone in the room to hear.

"Well," said Kellen's mom, "I can certainly see why Kellen doesn't want to watch that! I can't imagine what he could possibly learn from a singing calculator."

"It's more than—"

Cassie's mom interrupted. "All I know is that last year, at her old school, Cassie used to love her classes. Now all I hear is her complaining that they have to watch this show. And apparently the drama teacher has

CASSIE'S MOM

197

been replaced by a cafeteria worker? What is going on?"

"Uh . . . I have no idea what you're talking about," sputtered Rabbski.

"Well, maybe you'd better GET an idea!"

"Uh . . . I just . . ."

There was an awkward pause.

"When I was in school," said Quavondo's mom, "I had some very wonderful teachers who gave me a love of learning that has lasted my whole life. How is anyone going to get that from this TV show?"

"Hear, hear!" said Harvey's mom. "What I can't understand is why my son's chorus class was canceled and replaced with a singing calculator. He can certainly sing better than that calculator!"

My note: Truthfully, I prefer the calculator!

"Ms. Rabbski," said Sara's mom, "if the purpose of this meeting was to get us to

tell our children to be good little boys and girls and sit and listen to that nonsense every day, then I'm afraid you have failed to convince me."

"Me too," said some of the other parents.

My dad didn't say anything. But at least he had stopped checking his phone.

Rabbski paused a moment. It felt sort of like a time bomb was about to go off. Her fingers were twitching like she wished she had brought her Rubik's Cube. But she pulled herself together.

"Okay," she said. "Okay, this has been helpful. This gives me some good input to take back to the school board. I'll share your input with them and see what we can come up with. Maybe . . . maybe there is another solution."

We all looked at one another but tried really hard to play it cool. But we knew that we—the Origami Rebel Alliance—had finally won our first battle.

Harvey's Comment

So, who turned on the TV? And don't say origami Yoda, or I'll clobber you.

My Comment: No, it wasn't Origami Yoda. It was the surprise attack of . . .

JABBA THE PUPPETT!

BY KELLEN (AND TRANSCRIBED BY TOMMY)

The day after that meeting with our parents, we still had to go to FunTime class. We may have won a battle, but the war wasn't over. Rabbski told our parents she was going to take their concerns to the school board. Apparently, she hadn't done that by the time first period started . . .

Anyway, when it was time for Mr. Howell to turn on the TV, he pointed the remote at the TV and turned it on. Just like every day. EXCEPT . . . where had he gotten the remote from? Last night at the meeting, Rabbski couldn't find it anywhere!

"Where'd you find the remote, Mr. Howell?" I asked.

"Oh, didn't you know, Kellen?"

"Know what?"

Okay . . .

Now hold on . . .

This is going to blow your mind . . .

Howell pulled an Origami Jabba from his suit pocket.

"Mah bukkee, meya gakkalok FunTime, too! Mwa-ha-ha!"

Tommy and I jumped out of our seats and ran up to look at the Jabba. It was pretty good!

"Oh, yes," said Mr. Howell. "I know all about your Howell the Hutt. Pretty fitting, actually! He was always my favorite character. I like his style . . ."

"Mwaaa-ha-ha-ha!" laughed Jabba.

"Does this mean you're joining our Origami Rebel Alliance?" Tommy asked.

REMEMBER?
THERE IS A
RESEMBLANCE!

"Mwaaa-ha-ha!" This time it was Howell himself laughing. Then he suddenly stopped and said, "Of course not. But we do appear to have a common enemy . . . Now sit down, shut up, and watch the singing calculator!"

Harvey's Comment

WOW! ←

My Comment: Yep, wow!

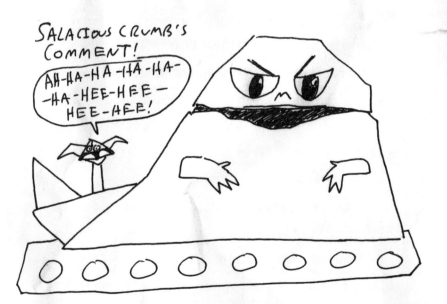

SALACIOUS CRUMB'S COMMENT!
AH-HA-HA-HA-HA-HA-HEE-HEE-HEE-HEE!

IT'S NOT OVER YET . . .

BY TOMMY

So . . . the next morning everybody—except poor old Mike—met in the library for a victory celebration. A fairly quiet one, of course, so there was no yub nub Ewok Dance.

At first there was a lot of "That was awesome" and "That was like getting free plastic dinosaurs!"

But then Harvey said, "You know, if I was Princess Leia, instead of Anakin—"

"And you ARE," said Kellen.

"If I may continue," said Harvey, "I

LIBRARY
RULE #39:
NO EWOK
DANCING!

NUB YUB!?

think I know what Princess Leia would say about this: "'That was TOO easy.'"

"Easy? You call that easy?" said Han Foldo/Sara.

"Thank you, Sara," said Harvey. "I knew you'd know what to say. And, yes, I do think that was TOO easy. Empress Rabbski isn't just going to give up! We can't stop now; we have to totally defeat her!"

"Right you are," said Origami Yoda, "and wrong."

"I thought Paperwad Yoda had finally gone away!" snapped Harvey.

"No longer your leader am I," said Origami Yoda. "But help you I will when I can."

"What about Dwight?" I asked.

"Purple," murmured Dwight, who had Origami Yoda on his left hand and was doing his math homework with his right hand.

"Right Harvey is that the fight is not

yet over," said Origami Yoda. "But you are wrong to think Rabbski is our enemy. She never has been . . ."

"WHAT????" said everyone.

"Never on the Dark Side has Rabbski been. Always wanted to help us she did, and help us she may even now . . ."

"Help us?" I said. "Don't you remember how Empress Rabbski 'helped' you get kicked out of school last year?!"

"Hrmmm . . . Mistakes she has made . . . but great forces are pushing against her from above. The Empress she is not. Like us she is but a pawn in a great game."

"He's right," said Amy. "FunTime was dumped on us by the school board, just like Rabbski said. And the school board is just trying to deal with state regulations. And the state laws got passed because of federal laws from Washington, D.C.!"

"Wug," groaned Chewie.

"Well . . . nostrul . . . ," said Kellen.

"Why didn't you tell us this earlier??? There's no way we can fight something that big!"

"Judge us by our size do you, hrmmmm?" asked Origami Yoda. "Hrmm? Hrmm?"

"Uh . . . no?" muttered Kellen.

"And well you should not," said Yoda. "The Force is strong with us! Win this we can!"

And then Origami Yoda turned and looked at me.

"Win this we must!"

"Uh, why are you pointing him at me, Captain Dwight?" I asked.

"It's just Dwight," said Dwight.

"Okay," I said. "Why is Origami Yoda looking at me, Dwight?"

"Probably because you and Foldy-Wan are supposed to lead the Rebel Alliance from now on!"

"But I can't!" I said.

"MUST!" said Origami Yoda. "Only YOU can lead this rebellion to victory. Your destiny it is . . . ."

"No way!" said Harvey, and probably everybody else was thinking it, too, because I definitely was.

"Way yes," said Origami Yoda.

TO BE CONTINUED

How To Fold The Poppett!

BY...?

INSTRUX BY KELLEN

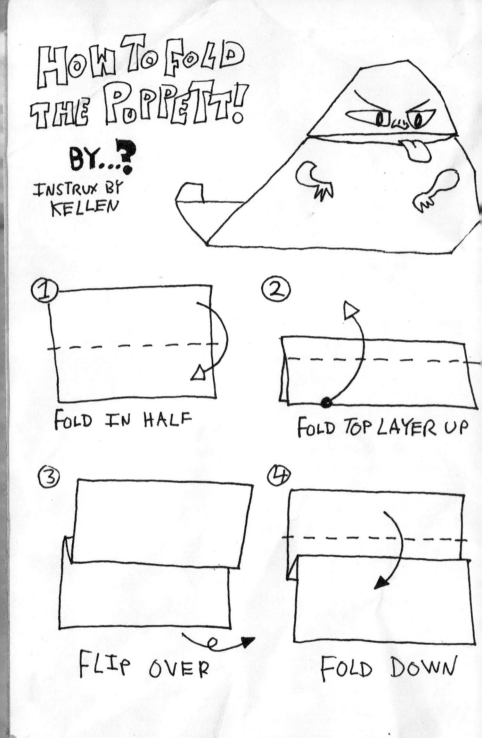

① FOLD IN HALF

② FOLD TOP LAYER UP

③ FLIP OVER

④ FOLD DOWN

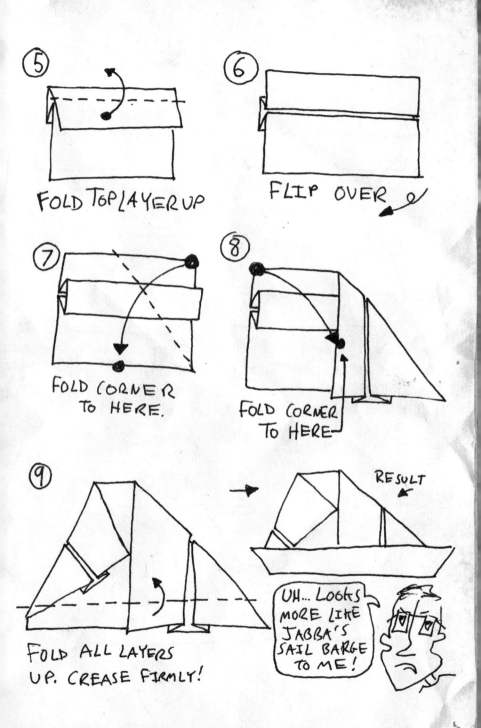

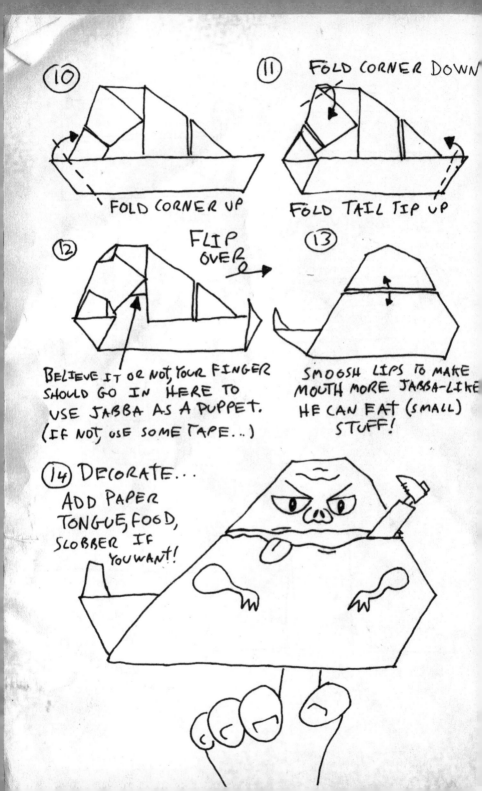

(10)

FOLD CORNER UP

(11) FOLD CORNER DOWN

FOLD TAIL TIP UP

(12)

FLIP OVER

BELIEVE IT OR NOT, YOUR FINGER SHOULD GO IN HERE TO USE JABBA AS A PUPPET. (IF NOT, USE SOME TAPE...)

(13)

SMOOSH LIPS TO MAKE MOUTH MORE JABBA-LIKE HE CAN EAT (SMALL) STUFF!

(14) DECORATE...
ADD PAPER
TONGUE, FOOD,
SLOBBER IF
YOU WANT!

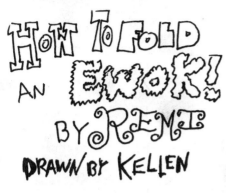

HOW TO FOLD AN EWOK!
BY REMI
DRAWN BY KELLEN

I'M KIRIGAMI!

NO SCISSORS NEEDED!

①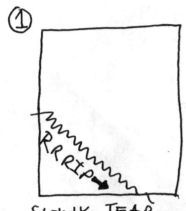

RRRIP➔

SLOWLY TEAR AWAY A BIG TRIANGLE ON LEFT SIDE

②

RRIP➔

TEAR AWAY A TRIANGLE ON RIGHT

③

X

USE PEN TO POKE HOLE

④ USE FINGER TO MAKE HOLE INTO A NICE FAT CIRCLE!

TEAR OFF EXTRA BITS

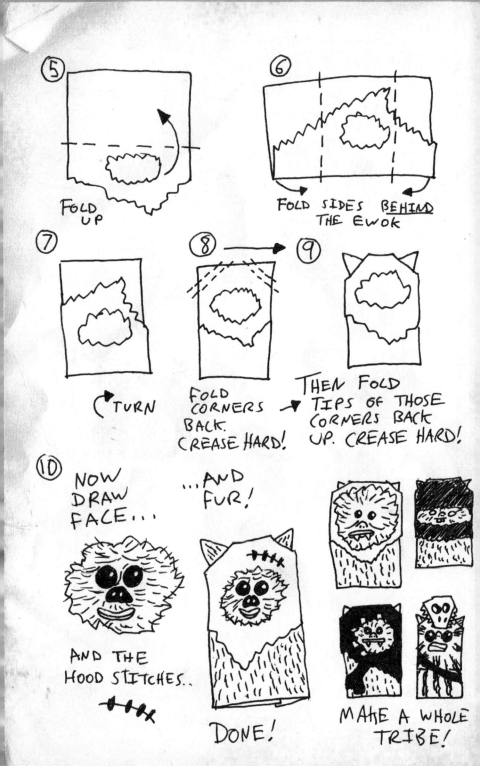

ACKNOWLEDGMENTS

Thank you, SuperFolders, SuperDoodlers,
SuperMovieMakers, the SuperFolderCouncil, and
SuperEverybodyElse who has added to origamiyoda.com!
(Sorry I couldn't put in all your names this time.
But you know that I couldn't/wouldn't do this without
you!) And Micah and Marcus: May the Force
be with you . . . Always.

Thank you, Caryn Wiseman, Michelle Weiner,
and everyone at Andrea Brown!

Thank you, Abrams and Amulet, where Susan, Chad,
Michael, Melissa, Jason, Steve, Erica, Jim,
Elisa, Mary, Marty, and Laura do so much for
me and the books.

Thank you, Scholastic, Scholastic Bookfairs,
and Recorded Books!

Thank you, sales reps and bookstore folks!

Thank you, librarians, library assistants, teachers,
reading specialists, principals, and assistant
principals!

Thank you, Hemphills, Team Rosenlaz, Mark Turetsky,
Jason Rosenstock, Webmaster Sam, Brian Compton, TJ,
Linda, Judy, Carla, Olga, Patti, Mrs. O'Brien, Colby,
The NerdyBookClub, and all my good old Kidlit pals and
some new ones: Raina & Dave, Tony & Ang, Jarret K.,
Tim Federle and Dav Pilkey!

And thank you to my parents, my family, and my
constant collaborator, Cece Bell!

ABOUT THE AUTHOR

TOM ANGLEBERGER is the author of the *New York Times* bestselling Origami Yoda series. He is also the author of *Fake Mustache* and *Horton Halfpott*, both Edgar Award nominees. He lives in the Appalachian Mountains of Virginia with his wife. Visit him online at www.origamiyoda.com.

This book was designed by Melissa J. Arnst and art directed by Chad W. Beckerman. The main text is set in 10-point Lucida Sans Typewriter. The display typeface is ERASER. Tommy's comments are set in Kienan, and Harvey's comments are set in Good Dog. The hand lettering on the cover was done by Jason Rosenstock.